IMELDA AND FRIENDS

a novel by
Peter Breschard

also by Peter Breschard

DEAD LEPERS
IN THE WIND

GALLDUBH PRESS
4584 SENECA DRIVE
OKEMOS, MI 48864
GALLDUBH@AOL.COM

Contents

LIGHTS

In northwestern Massachusetts, U.S.A.P.S., snow lethargically descends as Big Aloysius wraps his scarf tight against his collar. An enormous dog races down a twilit field towards shimmering purple lights a quarter mile away.

-Another damn machine.-

Big Aloysius goes back to what he's been doing. It's the rare day in early Spring when temperatures moderate enough for Big Aloysius to enjoy his favorite occupation. Digging grubs isn't neat work any time of year but permafrost makes this particular avocation downright impossible.

-Stupid mutt. When'll it learn.-

As more inches of dirt dislodge, Big Aloysius discloses another of this world's great delicacies. He pops the creature into his mouth savoring its variety of flavors as practically pure protein passes through his digestive system. Never too cold to enjoy good grub.

The enormous dog stares as lights hover twenty feet above him. To the dog, the lights signify nothing more than the chance to scrounge edible scraps from another group of tourists who occasionally wander into the section of woods he and his master claim as their own. Scrounging a satisfying meal has become the dog's primary goal since master now prefers a diet featuring predominantly subterranean cuisine.

The lights, which moments before appeared content to roam about the landscape randomly, suddenly focus their attention on one oversize dog, who responds with ferocious growls. His vocalization is cut short as the hound and his immediate surroundings are entirely bathed in intense illumination. This illumination soon ceases. Again, darkness and silence.

Vram	Interesting.
Batbat	Not very interesting.
Vram	I mean interesting in an interesting way. From what I've ascertained, this isn't a rare specimen.
Batbat	It's a damn dog.
Vram	I'm aware it's a damn dog. I'm aware we have any number of more important species to study but, for the moment, we're here and, for the moment, the dog is here, so, for the moment, I propose we make creative use of the downtime you've so cleverly arranged for us, and examine this delightful doggie.
Batbat	It's a damn dog and we are explicitly not authorized to perform research involving indigenous life forms.
Vram	True. However, under the charter, we are empowered to use initiative if events come to pass which result in delay to our schedule. You do comprehend what I'm saying?

Batbat	This mess isn't my fault.
Vram	Who's assigning blame? Our situation could happen to anyone. So what if it happened to us? We didn't design the machine. We weren't the subcontractor who installed the drives. We weren't the ones responsible for routine maintenance. We operate the machine. I'm not blaming you for our present situation.
Batbat	Damn straight you're not.
Vram	Some periodic checks now and then might have helped.
Batbat	What are you talking about?
Vram	Oh, nothing.
Batbat	If you've something to say, say it. In the six years we've been together, never once have you said anything the easy way. No, you cozy the edges. You approach the subject from the side. Understatement. Metaphor. Sarcasm. You know how it makes me crazy.
Vram	No need getting riled.
Batbat	I'm not riled. If you've something to say concerning the way I've maintained this machine, I'd appreciate it if you, for once, told me straight out what the problem is. It would save me all the time I usually waste trying to figure out what's bugging you.
Vram	Beautiful night, isn't it?
Batbat	Come on. Say it and get it over. You think I'm to blame for our dropping out of orbit and having to put in for repairs. If that's your conclusion, why don't you say so?

Vram	You're to blame for our dropping out of orbit and having to put in for repairs.
Batbat	There you go again. I know what you're thinking and you refuse to say it.
Vram	You're to blame for our dropping out of orbit and having to put in for repairs.
Batbat	Fine. Would you mind telling me what's on your mind? Listening to you banter along gets me if you go on for too long.
Vram	The dog.
Batbat	Out of the question. We've been banned from fiddling with indigenous personnel.
Vram	Nobody would know.
Batbat	Everybody would know. There's no way to keep it secret.
Vram	But we've got it. We could modify it. It would work.
Batbat	You haven't the slightest idea how much trouble this could cause us.
Vram	It'd be fun. We don't know how long we'll be stuck here.
Batbat	Unfortunately, you're on the money on that one.
Vram	If we're here for an extended period of time and don't do anything productive, we could lose our commissions.
Batbat	We won't be here so long.
Vram	We could use a control group.
Batbat	What?
Vram	A control group. We'd duplicate it and miniaturize it. It's easy. Should only take a couple of days.
Batbat	I don't like this.

Vram We can't sit here, hope the ship repairs itself and do absolutely nothing.

Batbat I'll have to log it as your idea.

Vram Fine. If it works I'll give you some of the credit.

Batbat I still don't know.

Vram Take a shot. We've nothing to lose.

There is a short passage of time while a decision is carefully considered and eventually made.

Batbat O.K., but you have to feed the dog and take it out for walks. If the operations aren't successful, I'm not helping you dig any holes.

OUT OF THE FOREST

In a tiny house in a tiny forest, a compact human entity lives all by her lonesome. Except for her cat. Except for people who live down the road not far away. Except for amiable animals who live in homes near the tiny cabin where the compact human entity lives. She lives all alone except for people she sees each and every day when she goes into town to do things one does when one goes into town to do things one must do when one goes into town. Other than people she sees every day and people who live close by and amiable animals who live in homes near her house, the compact human entity lives all alone. Except for her cat. Who recently was discovered by a major advertising agency, signed on as a national spokescat and moved to the big city.

Early one late afternoon while walking home from town on the road through the forest and very, very close to her house, the compact human entity hears a new and different noise coming from the forest. Not being a type of compact human entity to run into the forest every time she hears a sound not familiar to her, she stands very still on the road and ponders.

"Maybe if I stand here a while, I'll figure out what type of sound the sound is. I might even find what strange thing makes a such strange sound. Or if I wait very quietly, maybe I'll hear the sound again."

So the compact human entity waits on the side of the road hoping to hear the noise again, the entire time trying to imagine what type of animal, vegetable or mineral creates such a strange sound.

Being the compact human entity the compact human entity is, the compact human entity stands very still by the side of the road for a very long time. As the sun starts to go down behind the end of the road (the compact human entity is facing due west at this time), the compact human entity begins wondering if she will ever figure out what made the strange sound and if she will ever hear the strange sound again. As the sun disappears beneath the horizon and the temperature drops, the compact human entity has doubts concerning her original idea of waiting exactly where she is standing and remaining very quiet in hope of understanding what the strange sound she heard actually is.

With the sky darkening and the temperature becoming colder and colder with every passing minute, the compact human entity wonders if the thin cotton blouse she has on will be able to withstand the freezing temperatures, an omnipresent climactic condition for this part of the country once the sun goes down beneath the road.

As the compact human entity shivers while maintaining her solitary vigil by the side of the road, we'll take a moment here to move thirty yards due south of the compact human entity by the side of the road to see if we can discover what the origin of the curious sound which seemingly precipitated neo-cranial paralysis in what this symposium will consider a somewhat typical human, female, North American subject.

> *"They are holy angels upon the earth, authors of good, averters of evil, the guardians of speech-gifted men."*
>
> Plato

INTO THE FOREST

Into the forest. A clearing lies ahead. A meadow created by some long-dead dirt farmer. Nothing grows there other than short weeds which now occupy 97.9% of its space. The other 2.1% of the area appears covered by a human subject, male, post-mature adult, North American subject and, at the moment, an indescribable piece of machinery which the subject appears to manipulate with class-R digitally controlled devices common to this area.

* Subject examines a "hand tool" utilizing dual ocular organs.
* Subject lowers cranium and presumably examines lower extremities sheathed within shards of processed dead animal carcasses.
* Subject launches "hand tool" into low parabolic arc. "Hand tool" travels a linear distance equal to 35% of cleared area prior to impact.

"Piece of garbage." Big Aloysius looks at his shoes once again and whispers to himself, "What a bunch of fool you are." Big Aloysius stirs up some dirt with his right toe and walks away from what appears to be a jury-rigged piece of machinery. He crosses the meadow to retrieve the pipe wrench he hastily attempted to launch into orbit moments before.

As Big Aloysius leans over the semi-submerged pipe wrench, he hears a sneeze from somewhere in the trees due north of where he now stands. Having spent a major portion of his life alone in this forest, Big Aloysius has developed a range of senses which many might consider well beyond those available to men and women, and similar to those of non-domestic animals. For a long time Big Aloysius had a friend in the forest. His friend's name was Little Aloysius and Little Aloysius was a dog.

Big Aloysius and Little Aloysius would often roam the forest for days and days without hearing anything other than the sounds which come from those animals who live in the forest on a regular basis and don't come to the forest as a "seasonal thing". Big Aloysius dislikes the summer since it is during the summer when the odd ones who usually don't spend any time at all in the forest come to the forest and ride through the forest on machines which make an excess of noise, causing both Big Aloysius and Little Aloysius to become exceedingly cranky.

Big Aloysius and Little Aloysius often sat together in a very still way and competed against each other to see which one could hear the sounds of the machines before the other. Whenever one of them would hear the noisy machines he would start running in the direction of the noise. If Big Aloysius heard the machine first, Big Aloysius had a chance of spotting the machine first. If Little Aloysius heard the machine first, Big Aloysius never had a chance of spotting the machine first. Little Aloysius is a very fast dog. Big Aloysius being so much taller than Little Aloysius doesn't help.

One day while Big Aloysius and Little Aloysius were enjoying their game, seeing who can hear, then see, the noisy machines first, Little Aloysius runs so fast he leaves Big Aloysius a long way behind in the forest. Big Aloysius looks everywhere he can for Little Aloysius but Big Aloysius cannot find his friend no matter where he looks.

Big Aloysius searches throughout the long day and stops to rest only when the sun has been away for many hours and Big Aloysius can no longer walk in the forest without tripping over everything he can't see since it is now exceptionally dark. As Big Aloysius rests his head on a soft log, Big Aloysius thinks he hears Little Aloysius barking somewhere in the forest. Big Aloysius wants to get up and find Little Aloysius but Big Aloysius realizes Little Aloysius is far away and Big Aloysius won't be able to find Little Aloysius in the darkness since Big Aloysius keeps falling down whenever he attempts walking more than two steps, it now being so exceptionally dark in the forest. Big Aloysius goes to sleep dreaming he will reunite with Little Aloysius the next morning. As Big Aloysius falls asleep thinking he will rejoin Little Aloysius the next morning, Big Aloysius hears the sounds of a noisy machine.

For many months Big Aloysius wanders the forest looking everywhere he possibly can imagine for Little Aloysius. Big Aloysius even looks under fallen trees. Big Aloysius even looks under stacks of leaves. Big Aloysius even looks anyplace he hasn't looked before and often even looks in places where he already has looked. He never does find Little Aloysius. But he does find one of the noisy machines.

Silence. Words never written soar across the stratosphere. Every night Big Aloysius hunkers his haunches up the nearest tree deemed capable of supporting his weight.

Big Aloysius prefers the ground. Little Aloysius would stand guard while they slept. But Little Aloysius has sunk his teeth into the ultimate tire of truth and spun his destiny wheel into the canine constellations. With the ground taken from beneath his feet, Big Aloysius each evening creates his own island in the sky from where, on clear mornings, he sees the wheeled invaders, but never his dear Little Aloysius.

ITEMS FOR MONDAY'S SYMPOSIUM

* Simian behavior vs. Homo sapiens' terra firma tendencies.
* The effects of 0-degree temperatures on inert Homo sapiens.
* Commercial responsibility for maintaining post sanitation, vis-a-vis non-kenneled canine specimens and proper disposal of their waste products.

BARNEY RUBBLE THUMBTACKS

Professor Radigan rises from his platform bed. He unpins a sheet covering the window and 1,000 lumens psi engulf the room. Maybe 1,001. He tacks the sheet to the windowsill using Barney Rubble thumb tacks, left over from a visit by his brother, sister-in-law and three nephews, formulating a fashion statement never to be seen in the pages of any popular magazine.

Radigan has staked out his own piece of the universe which he now shares in ownership with a major bank, three mortgage brokerage houses, a non-retired widow from another redundant suburb, and a pension fund from a union formerly associated with organized crime and now involved with renovating low income urban housing in connection with some extremely well off ex-Washington bureaucrats formerly affiliated with the Department of Housing and Urban Development, most of whose co-workers recently transferred to numerous Federal institutions of minimum security rehabilitation.

Radigan sits at the computer and connects with WEB. This ethernet appears especially well named since Radigan finds nothing in the tangled public access area of interest. He shifts gears, accessing more sophisticated levels of WEB.

Various studies, a few academic in-jokes and gossip, ecological mood-swing observations, higher level bulletin board members seeking contact with lost colleagues. Recipes for macrobiotic algorithms.

Radigan scans the messages of the past two weeks. He knows he's been away too long but moving into new digs remains a project which completely shuts down any other systems until Radigan feels enough at ease to wake up in the morning and immediately move to the console.

For the past two weeks, Radigan's been shifting between the old and the new. He thinned out his possessions and reordered his life. Radigan's moves never affect his life to any noticeable extent but Romantic nomadism keeps him from believing his ideas stagnant. He supposes himself more receptive to innovative concepts when compelled to manipulate a new plumbing system or neighborhood. Questions from junior faculty members at the lab never seem as inane when Radigan is befuddled by the operation of an unfamiliar garbage disposal at home. Aside from this, after a year or two his neighbors start wondering why the new guy still acts so oddly, moving boxes around in the middle of the night.

WEB must have come from somewhere even though Radigan knows there can't be any mastermind behind this electronic organization. It's as if an inconceivable number of bees from completely different parts of the world, who buzz in entirely different bee languages, decided to shift locations simultaneously. The bees took off from their various hives and flew in any direction they chose. Some north, some south, some east, some up, some down, some hover a bit then enter a passing jet's slipstream, ending up wherever the plane touches down. Simply put, complete randomization.

Now, when the native bees meet these alien bees, who live in a hive in some neck of the woods where no bee has ever seen a bee like the one recently dropped from some transient 727, the new bees are greeted with skepticism. But when the native bees realize a few bees from their own hive might be sitting on the bumper of a semi-tractor trailer heading down the road to who-knows-where, they allow the alien bees to work alongside them in the hive, especially since hives worldwide were standardized millennia ago and, even if most of the alien bees are used to metric sized cells, they rapidly adapt.

Now hives throughout the world are working in a manner never before seen anywhere. Bees take a little from here, a little from there, and soon, although it may appear to a bee who's been hibernating on Rip Van Winkle's nose for a couple of decades that all the hives have fallen into complete chaos, in reality the hives are working at a level of productivity immeasurable by the various hives which instead of making honey spend their time figuring out which hives are the most cost/labor effective in the production process.

Radigan knew these hives are now linked together through the use of two A.M. phone lines. Any hive which wants to can find out what's happening in any other hive, production schedules, flavors, bee-power allocations, production reports, etc., by directly tapping into a distant hive's computer. No longer do these numerous hives need to support selected hives which produce nothing aside from figures and summations of what various hives are doing. Drones now communicate only with other drones.

Radigan worries about this. For years he's been on the edge. He would work at one of the productive hives for a bit, then he'd shift to a research/analysis hive where the only task he was assigned was to count beans. Only now does he catch on to this underground river of information that's been flowing under his nose the past few years. But Radigan has always been a quick study and feels confident he'll land on his feet when the day comes for the shift.

Already Radigan sees changes in his everyday existence. Clerks in bodegas who aren't really working where they appear to be working. Gas pump jockeys who might as well be writing their PhD thesis as they note your driver's license number on the back of your check.

A TRADITIONAL EDUCATION

There was a time, or was it another time, when the compact human entity would never have considered being stuck in the middle of a country road as snow begins to fall. During this other time she would have thrust her chin and chest forward, put one foot resolutely in front of the other and attacked such an inadequate challenge as mere flakes with the determination born of seeing every film ever made starring Katherine Hepburn. But that time isn't this time and this time the compact human entity thinks it best to stay very still as the snowflakes amass and the inches of snow grow to feet about her.

The compact human entity takes her increasing immobility with the style, grace and dignity she's accustomed to taking to such everyday inconveniences as long lines in grocery stores, delivery men's muddy shoes, someone hiccuping at the opera or, horror of horrors, a Spring wearing Fall colors who someone praises for daring color sense. Piffle and nonsense. The snow continues to pile up.

Once, when the compact human entity was an even more compact human entity, an older boy took her to the seashore so they could live where the sun shines every day, nobody is permitted to frown, everyone must be good looking, none of the natives speak Spanish, and the University of Southern California offers a doctoral degree in mall shopping for students for whom English or Spanish is a second language.

Finding herself in a beautiful Beverly Hills mall, the older boy gives her some cards and tells her to enjoy herself while he goes off to his regularly scheduled aerobic/ powerlifting class. The compact human entity cannot believe such good fortune to be truly hers. She looks three hundred and fifty-two degrees around at the many and varied wonderful shops filled with everything designed to give Imelda Marcos a carnal dream, and knows this is where she belongs.

The compact human entity goes to the middle of the mall, closes her eyes, spins her body around on her right toe, and when she feels she has spun her body around as much as she can without attracting too much attention and is totally unaware of the direction she faces, the compact human entity raises her right arm, points her index finger straight ahead, opens her eyes and gazes upon the store where she will soon make her first purchase. Isn't life grand!

And it's a wonderful boutique to discover. On entering, the compact human entity imagines she has stumbled onto the backstage of a road company production of "The Glass Menagerie" but, when the compact human entity regains her bearings and examines the ever so tiny price tags attached to the ever so tiny items the shop has for sale, the compact human entity knows for a fact she must be in a never-never land where the only way you can return home is if the person at the other end of the telephone, when the clerk checks your credit rating, suggests to your clerk that they take out a pair of their sharpest scissors and put a little hole in the plastic balloon you're attempting to kite at the moment. The compact human entity never, ever wants this happening to her. Nosiree.

And it's not going to happen. The compact human entity unexpectedly realizes the rectangles of plastic in her hands are traps. Each time the compact human entity uses one of these cards she owes someone: the slightly older boy, the person who owns the store, the company who sends out millions of these pretty plastic cards, some bank in a big city, most probably not Los Angeles, or the shabby looking man the compact human entity sees walking on the other side of the street across from the store where she has these thoughts.

He isn't dressed the way anyone the compact human entity has previously observed in Beverly Hills dresses. He looks like someone from a news broadcast the compact human entity saw while switching television channels from game show starring the woman with the unlimited wardrobe flipping cards which seem to move by themselves and the quiz show which usually features three dreary men who know questions to answers the compact human entity would never begin to question but the compact human entity likes to know what the big brains look like. They look remarkably the same.

Even the rare women who sometimes are among the three dreary men all look like they'd rather be slinging hash in a diner somewhere east of Elko, Texas, where the customers would be appreciative of their natural wit and intelligence rather than their having to dress like men who don't have any color sense and memorize silly facts they will use for only one day in their life as dreary people compete against the woman with the unlimited wardrobe who flips cards even though it looks like the cards could easily flip themselves.

News. News. News. The compact human entity can't understand why someone hurting someone else is news. The compact human entity can't comprehend why men dressed ostentatiously in green, running through some jungle or another while carrying rifles, is news. The compact human entity can't fathom why the same house burning down every day at six forty-five in the evening is news. Now and then, if the compact human entity has been playing outside and gotten colder than she planned and wants to get real warm, real fast and the time is a little before six forty-five in the evening, the compact human entity turns on one of the many local television stations where she knows she can warm her hands and her backside in front of the six forty-five fire. After turning up the thermostat, the compact human entity walks over to the television, turns it on, and as she rubs her hands in front of the screen, the compact human entity soon becomes warmer. The compact human entity guesses the news contains a single redeeming social element.

Now, the compact human entity remembers why the shabbily dressed man standing across the street looks familiar but the compact human entity can't recall ever seeing the dog before. But the dog isn't wearing any clothes, so the dog is harder to remember.

Big Aloysius knows he's in a different town but for some reason he has no idea how he found himself here. The last thing Big Aloysius remembers was going to sleep in the limbs of a very large tree after spending an entire night searching for Little Aloysius. Now he stands on the sidewalk in the middle of what Big Aloysius considers a sizable city. Traffic zips around him from countless directions. The few people walking the street look at him in a peculiar way. The sun is unendurably hot, and Little Aloysius again stands beside him. At least Big Aloysius is familiar with something.

Little Aloysius seems happy. Big Aloysius squats down and gives Little Aloysius the kind of hug only the owner of a dog who thought he'd lost his dog forever can give to a dog he thought he'd lost forever.

This isn't the first time, and probably won't be the last time, Big Aloysius thought Little Aloysius was lost forever and ever. Big Aloysius remembers a day which seems long ago when he was walking on the side of the road looking for Little Aloysius whom Big Aloysius thought was lost forever when a stranger at the wheel of one of the largest, noisiest, smokiest vehicles Big Aloysius had ever seen pulls up in front of Big Aloysius and, stepping down from a throne Big Aloysius can barely see, the throne stands so high above the side of the road where Big Aloysius is walking, walks back to where Big Aloysius stands on the side of the road, and stops only a few feet in front of Big Aloysius.

"Do you know where I am?" was the question the man asked.

Rather than give the man from the enormous vehicle an obvious answer, "Yes, you're standing in front of me." Big Aloysius, who never enjoys using one word when none will do, simply nods his head and points in the direction of the man, to indicate that Big Aloysius knows exactly where the man is. Words too often lead to too much miscommunication for Big Aloysius's taste and Big Aloysius finds drawing a map or pointing a finger usually does the trick.

Obviously, the driver of this smoky vehicle has been on driving far too long and undoubtedly quaffed too much caffeine or ingested too many other substances designed to keep the driver awake and mentally alert which they are obviously doing since the driver immediately grasps what Big Aloysius is communicating.

The driver turns away from Big Aloysius and looks past himself down the road in the direction his vehicle already faces. Then the driver turns back to Big Aloysius.

"You know, that's what I thought. It's only in these backwoods, I get a bit confused as to what direction I'm heading. Every now and then I need to stop and get a second opinion. Thanks, buddy."

And the driver sticks out his right hand to Big Aloysius. Big Aloysius remembering exactly what to do in this exact situation, sticks his right hand out to the driver and the two hands clasp one another in memory of the wonderful instant of fellowship, exchange of knowledge, and good times, these two human beings have shared.

The driver walks back to his vehicle. But, as the driver takes the first step up to the throne of his enormous, smoky machine, he turns back to Big Aloysius and waving his right arm shouts, "Hey, buddy, how about I give you a lift?"

At the moment the fact that Big Aloysius is on the side of the road looking for Little Aloysius whom Big Aloysius assumes lost forever, depresses Big Aloysius a great deal. Little Aloysius has been lost many times before but each time Big Aloysius assumes Little Aloysius lost forever. Big Aloysius remains depressed. Big Aloysius certainly could use a lift so Big Aloysius follows the beckoning arm of the driver and soon climbs high above the side of the road to rest upon a throne very much like the driver's. Rolling down the road in the truck, Big Aloysius has never before been able to cover so much territory in his search for Little Aloysius so fast. Big Aloysius hasn't seen this many trees in an inordinately long time.

"So, buddy, where about you want me to take you?"

Big Aloysius only wants to be is in the same place as Little Aloysius but, since Big Aloysius doesn't know where Little Aloysius resides at the moment, the only way Big Aloysius can reply to the driver's question is with a shrug. Big Aloysius doesn't know where Little Aloysius is. Little Aloysius could be anywhere.

"Alright, buddy. Always glad to meet another knight of the highway. You sit back and enjoy the ride. We're straight down the road a ways. You let me know."

And since Big Aloysius doesn't know, the two of them keep spinning down the highway.

Big Aloysius always enjoys travelling down any road whether it's walking down the side of a country highway or highballing it in the middle of a multi-lane transcontinental freeway while sitting atop the throne of a semi-tractor trailer with eighteen wheels, portable generator, two bunks in the back, television, VCR, CD, shower, sink, toilet, fax machine; Compaq 8000-gig, hard driving, 986, 1600mhz, moused, modemed, Ultra-Super VGA 23" monitor, color laser printered personnel computer; ice box, and double burner cooker.

Every fifteen miles or thereabouts the driver takes a taste of a cola which makes Big Aloysius, when he tastes some, feel edgy and jumpingly wide awake. The driver speaks for a hundred miles at a clip, seeming never to pause for breath. When the two of them eventually reach the interstate, the driver keeps his rig in the middle lane and maintains a speed which means most of the cars in front of him soon change lanes when they find an eighteen wheel semi-tractor trailer six inches from their rear bumper.

And so, the driver and Big Aloysius, high above most other traffic, cruise the highway. Big Aloysius is constantly looking out his window trying to locate Little Aloysius but he never does. The driver has Big Aloysius hold the wheel steady while he goes into the rear compartment for a minute or two. Sometimes Big Aloysius uses the facilities himself.

The driver and Big Aloysius, high above most other traffic, cruise the highway, and with the exception of driving through a swarm of bees, some splattering against the windshield, some hitching a ride on the bumper, enjoy the long ride without incident.

SHOP SHOP

Imelda Marcos cannot believe she is where she is. This must be a dream. She knows the only thing she needs do to get home is tap the heels of her ruby slippers together three times, say "There's no place like home", and she will immediately be magically delivered back from whence she came. But there remains this one problem. When Imelda was forced to rush so very, very much, in order to catch her plane from Manila to Hawaii, she did not have time to properly pack the many pairs of ruby slippers she elegantly stored in her many closets.

Everyone was running around the presidential palace trying to find mates for single socks lost during the multiple years Imelda and What's-his-name occupied the palace. Imelda knew What's-his-name had no intention of vacating the presidential palace until each and every one of his socks found its mate. Imelda feels it would not be polite if she didn't at least help organize the search parties. Imelda loves just about every kind of party.

As rebel jets sporadically buzz the presidential palace, Imelda organizes her servants into search teams. The leader of the

"Hanes" group, consisting of two colonels, three majors, five upstairs maids, two cobblers, and a dozen NCO's, is General Oscar de Laleesa . (The General is mostly laughed at behind his own back, except for the odd occasion when forced to visit certain sections of New England in the United States of America and Points South where it is said a certain infamous former Speaker of the United States House of Representatives upon being introduced to the General was so overly bemused by the General's appearance and name that the former Speaker of the United States House of Representatives laughingly sprayed the General with half a pint of dark ale interspersed with a quarter pound of semi-chewed linguica which, unfortunately, was the contents of the former Speaker's mouth at the moment of introduction. As the former Speaker laughs and apologizes, the General, after examining his thoroughly besmirched uniform, walks back to Imelda Marcos who consoles the mightily upset general. Imelda immediately confronts the former Speaker of the United States House of Representatives with the immortal words, "You are a very, very fat and tasteless man. Yes, you are." Fortunately for the former Speaker, the events which began this part of the story are but a few weeks in the future and the former Speaker from Boston simply laughs some more.) General Oscar de Laleesa has the complete confidence of Her Fabness, Imelda Marcos.

The esteemed and gracious General of the Army of the Philippines and Surrounding Suburbs, Oscar de Laleesa, is again most honored by Her Swell Ladyship on his being appointed head of the "Hanes" search team. Sure, there are other search teams, but this is the "Hanes" group. How often has he listened to What's-his-name berate the so-called "sockless masses", which the General first assumes to be another new rite of the Catholic Church, but later comes to know What's-his-name means everyone without an account at Neiman-Marcus, Etc., Inc., Texas, U.S.A.P.S..

It had been a hard life for the General until dame fortune smiled upon him in the form of Her Most Stylish Madame President for Life (Unless There's a Massive Breakthrough in Cryogenics) of the Philippines and Surrounding Suburbs, Imelda Marcos.

Oscar de Laleesa, the General-to-be, was born to a ne'er-do-well family in the capital city of Manila. He is the third son of a once limousine-less investment banker whose only claim to fame consists of being second cousin once removed to the President for Life (Unless There's a Massive Breakthrough in Cryogenics) of the Philippines and Surrounding Suburbs, What's-his-name.

The General-to-be's parents had only enough money to send his two older brothers away to be educated in the United States of America and Points South. The General-to-be's eldest brother, Omar de Laleesa, attended Harvard, where, as an undergraduate economist, he appeared destined to return to the Philippines to continue the economic miracle begun by the President for Life (Unless There's a Massive Breakthrough in Cryogenics) of the Philippines and Surrounding Suburbs, What's-his-name. Unfortunately, one day while taking a break from his studies, the General-to-be's elder brother and some of his fraternity brothers, who, co-incidentally, were all blood relatives of various saviors of diminutive, quasi-democratic, freedom loving client states of the United States of America and Points South, decided to get a small taste of local culture and visit various neighborhood nightspots.

Entering a local tavern, the fraternity brothers, alive with collegial recklessness, soon down one beer and then another. As the evening wears on, the General-to-be's elder brother becomes enamored of two young women sitting at a booth across the room from the increasingly more sociable fraternity brothers. To the General-to-be's elder brother, the two young women appear as a vision sent directly from the gods. It's the General-to-be's elder brother's dream mail order wish. After many months of intense study in this strange land, spending night after night memorizing secret handshakes of investment bankers or boning up on the effect inflation has on Ralph Lauren's collection with a fraternity brother, who, surprisingly, happens to be the son of a lesser member of the House of Saud, and after spending hours before a mirror in an attempt not to look or sound silly while pronouncing the most elusive of American idioms, "Muffy", the General-to-be's elder brother is savagely prepared for social interaction.

Egged on by his fraternity brothers, fortified by their sage advice as to commoners being easier than real humans, aware his sports jacket alone would cost most Americans three weeks' salary, the General-to-be's elder brother dares crossing the few feet to the booth of his desire and introduce himself.

Unfortunately for the General-to-be's elder brother, both young women come from the same neighborhood as the previously mentioned former Speaker of the United States of America and Points South House of Representatives. Fortunately for the General-to-be's elder brother, the two young women are facing one another when he introduces himself as the Esteemed and Honorable Omar de Laleesa of the Philippines and Surrounding Suburbs and continues that he would very, very much appreciate having a meaningful relationship with the two of them back at his condo.

Laughter remains an incomparably curious fact of human existence. In the midst of constant oppression even those suffering from gross malnutrition can take a small part of the day to laugh.

It's a necessity. Laughter will forever be as necessary as breathing, only seeming less so, due to its irregularity. Omar de Laleesa always has matching socks and as a student of economics at a supposedly prestigious American university, he, if this can be possible, has less of a sense of humor than the President for Life (Unless There's a Massive Breakthrough in Cryogenics) of the Philippines and Surrounding Suburbs, What's-his-name.

Many young men take young women laughing at them grievously. Happens a lot. That's life. To give a fair paraphrase of a Georgian politician, "Nobody said life was `Peanuts'", but try telling this to a young frat brother who in his own country could have the two young women incarcerated for weeks as suspected communist subversives for behavior such as this.

The General's elder brother backs away from the young women's booth, embarrassingly bruised but slightly unbeaten.

Returning to his table, Omar de Laleesa feels pulverized. Facing an immature miniaturized version of the United Nations General Assembly, at first it appears to the General's elder brother that these blood relatives of the rich and powerful will fall back on their childhood training and maintain straight faces.

This isn't about to happen. Omar watches his mates' mugs turn from the ideal of diplomatic stoicism, to one or two handkerchiefs covering one or two mouths, to a few faces turning away, obviously interested in happenings elsewhere, to one snort, to two snorts, to one low spontaneously repressed giggle, to a short laugh, to a few short laughs, to a long laugh, to two long, loud laughs, to every one of his fraternity brothers sitting in the booth in this common bar in Boston, Massachusetts, U.S.A.P.S., thunderously chortling in the face of the Esteemed and Honorable Omar de Laleesa of the Philippines and Surrounding Suburbs.

The General-to-be's elder brother finds such behavior on the part of his peers intolerable, as well as extremely embarrassing. The Esteemed and Honorable Omar de Laleesa of the Philippines and Surrounding Suburbs turns his back on an ivy-covered United States of America and Points South education and purposefully strolls out of the bar.

The elder brother of the General-to-be drops completely out of sight for several years. The General-to-be's parents are deeply concerned but find themselves frustrated in their attempts to locate poor Omar. For five years they mourn their lost son until, finally, when they have all but totally given up hope of being reunited, they receive a three color brochure published by a real estate company located in Lake Tehatchiwatchit, Minnesota, U.S.A.P.S.. The top salesman for the real estate company is pictured with his family. Omar looks well, if a bit plump. His wife's face is a map of Nippon. The General-to-be's father tears the brochure to pieces and forbids everyone in the family from ever again speaking the name of the-one-who-is-forever-lost.

Fortunately for the family de Laleesa, the second son, Roberto, was more fortunate in his American undergraduate career. Eschewing "the great whore on the Charles", the General-to-be's parents send Roberto to that most significant of cultural institutions, the University of Southern California. Their logic being, if it's good enough for the indicted co-conspirators of Señor Richard, it will most certainly be adequate for Roberto.

Roberto finds the atmosphere at the University of Southern California even less egalitarian than at "the great whore on the Charles", which he visited while he and his father searched for poor the-one-who-is-forever-lost, and Roberto enjoys his stay at the University of Southern California immensely.

Eventually Roberto receives a doctoral degree in mall shopping for students for whom English or Spanish is a second language and returns to Manila, capital of the Philippines and Surrounding Suburbs, where Roberto opens his own chain of mini-malls, with ample parking for bicycles and pedicabs. Donut shops in every neighborhood is obviously an idea whose time has come in the Philippines and Surrounding Suburbs.

And so the family continues its hand-to-mouth existence, and when the time comes for the General-to-be to journey across the great water to enter a fine United States of America and Points South University as Roberto and the-one-who-is-forever-lost have done before him, the General-to-be packs his suitcase and awaits his father's return from the office to motor him to the airport where he will bid farewell to his beloved Manila, venturing into the strange and wonderful world which is the University of Southern California in majestic downtown Los Angeles, California, U.S.A.P.S., the de Laleesa family University of choice.

As his father's limousine approaches the house, the young General-to-be cannot restrain his joy. Running to the car as his father emerges, the General-to-be opens his arms to embrace his father. But, seeing his father's face, the General-to-be immediately realizes his hopes of moving to Minnesota and marrying a sweet Nipponese girl like the wife of the-one-who-is-forever-lost are lost.

Emerging from the car, the General-to-be's father stops in front of his youngest son and raises his right arm in military fashion.

"My dear son, Oscar, I salute you as the newest member of the Army of the Philippines and Surrounding Suburbs. You are to be appointed captain in the most esteemed palace guard of the President for Life (Unless There's a Massive Breakthrough in Cryogenics), What's-his-name."

Lowering his arm, the General-to-be's father extends his hand to the General-to-be. Father and captain shake hands for a moment. The moment is soon lost. The General-to-be's father speaks, "What's for dinner, son?"

Picking up his packed suitcases, the General-to-be follows his father into the house.

Later in the evening the General-to-be learns the true meaning of his captaincy in the Palace Guard of President for Life (Unless There's a Massive Breakthrough in Cryogenics) of the Philippines and Surrounding Suburbs, What's-his-name. The General-to-be's mother is enthused, elated, ecstatic and enraptured about the news. She exuberantly embraces her youngest son and tells the maid to throw away the meal which has been prepared. No, the family will celebrate this momentous occasion and a pork roast the cook spent most of the day preparing, along with the rest of the trimmings, is relegated to a dump outside Manila. Señora de Laleesa is instantaneously on the telephone to Roberto.

Within an hour, or well into the second bottle of vintage New York State, U.S.A.P.S., champagne, Roberto arrives at the front door. In the street behind Roberto are three delivery vans bearing the markings of a few of the many franchises Roberto de Laleesa has accumulated for his mini-malls.

And as Señora de Laleesa fusses about the dining room and the General-to-be, his father and brother drink to the prospect of the General-to-be's stellar future, the delivery men from the vans enter the de Laleesa home bearing the finest product American dining has to export. Truly a feast of wide divergence and, almost without saying, speed.

As the multi-uniformed caterers withdraw, the de Laleesa family arrays itself about the pure oak veneer dining room table to consume a feast few in the Philippines and Surrounding Suburbs can imagine, let alone afford.

Grouped in front of each de Laleesa are innumerable containers constructed either of cardboard or mystery plastic, frequently labeled with the colorful logos of their respective fast food chain of origin.

"Tonight we celebrate the elevation of our beloved son and brother, Oscar, to the most exalted palace guard of the President for Life (Unless There's a Massive Breakthrough in Cryogenics) of the Philippines and Surrounding Suburbs, What's-his-name." And following the General-to-be's father's toast, the de Laleesa family falls to it.

Hors d'oeuvres from Dunkin Donuts and Kentucky Fried Chicken. A fish course from the Scottish Restaurant. Salads entombed within clear plastic containers from everywhere. Individually wrapped pieces of sushi. Taco Bell fajitas with spices which truly stun Señora de Laleesa. Hamburgers, hotdogs, southern fried chicken, nibble sized pieces of spare ribs, chicken and several other unknown meats. Potato salad, coleslaw. Miniature sugared fruit pies. Milk shakes. A couple of things on a couple of sticks. Frozen yogurt. Ice cream treats mummified in five layers of paper and plastic. And many more individually wrapped concoctions which until the opening of Roberto's mini-malls were known only to those few citizens of the Philippines and Surrounding Suburbs having access to the high temple of American haute cuisine, the Army PX.

As the rest of the family continues its celebratory feast, Roberto wheels in three personnel entertainment centers, complete with 23" Zenith remote control televisions, Zenith stereo systems featuring multi-play CD's, and, of course, Zenith VCR's.

Roberto reseats himself. "And now for your dining entertainment..."

As the de Laleesa's chomp down on their feast of many franchises, they are entertained by some of the "thousands and thousands" of rock videos featured at Roberto's downtown Manila trendoid shop, "Hot Metal Vids for You and the Kids!", featuring pulsating everything, from prepubescents to garbage dumpsters, in and out of time, accompanied by up-to-the-minute synthesizers made in Korea.

But none of this satisfies the young General-to-be. Excusing himself from the table as Def Lepard segues into their one romantic ballad, the General-to-be slips up to his bedroom and stares for many minutes at his suitcases which will never know the beauty of a Minnesota mid-winter snowfall on a night when the moon shows full and the servants play banjos on the lawn while the General-to-be and his beautiful Nipponese bride sip pink piña coladas as they tranquilly doze in the gazebo.

The young General-to-be sadly moves his suitcases back onto their shelf in the closet and closes the door upon his dreams of America.

In the dining room, the family de Laleesa recognizes the sadness in young Oscar's eyes as he silently slips back into the dining room. Roberto, using his remote control, muzzles Motley Crue, then, with sympathetic eyes, he and Señora de Laleesa turn to the paterfamilias. The dejected General-to-be takes his seat as his father speaks.

"These are hard times for everyone alive today in the Philippines and Surrounding Suburbs, young Oscarino. On many of our islands the peasants curse the bounty they are given by us. Some young men, some younger then yourself, Oscar, have taken up with the atheistic, war loving, anti-family, anti-church, anti-property, antidisestablishmentterrianistic, lousy, rotten communists, and are terrorizing the terrorists we employ in those god forsaken islands. Wherever they are.

"So, my son, my possible General-to-be, I was faced with a simple choice. When I approached the Minister of Higher Education for Education in Foreign Countries Specifically the Southern Section of California, U.S.A.P.S., the Minister, the Minister himself, mind you, explained that unless this family were prepared to make even greater sacrifices than those for which we were already prepared, you would be drafted into the Army."

Roberto nods gloomily. "I expected better from cousin Jorge."

His father nods. "Not to blame cousin Jorge. He has been promoted to the English Public Boarding School Section of the Ministry. The man with whom I dealt was a virtual stranger, I believe him to be merely a third cousin of the President for Life (Unless There's a Massive Breakthrough in Cryogenics) of the Philippines and Surrounding Suburbs, What's-his-name, on his mother's side. Unfortunately, we are no relation."

The General-to-be looks up from his Quarter Pounder with Cheese. "Father, if I was to be drafted into the army, how did you manage to find me a captaincy in the most esteemed and honorable Palace Guard?"

"Son, my dear son, Oscarino, one thing you will learn in the years to come is that no man makes his way in this world alone." Señor de Laleesa smiles at his wife and Señora de Laleesa perks up appreciably.

"Having heard this morning such horrible news, I was thrown for a substantial loss. I knew the twenty thousand dollars we have already given the vice-chancellor of the mighty University of Southern California, so he might have a chance to obtain much needed cosmetic surgery for his wife, was gone forever. I attempted to offer comparable funds to the Minister but apparently some cousins must enter the army this month and the Minister is meeting enough medical expenses with contributions from his own side of the family to enable him to dismiss my attempt at persuasion. Your number was up.

"Feeling as forlorn as I have ever felt in my life, I telephoned your mother and relayed the bad news. For a moment, listening to your mother's silence, I believed everything we'd worked for for so many years was lost. Then your mother ordered me back home immediately. There's something which might help, she tells me.

"Being driven back here as fast as our fool chauffeur can drive, my heart was at a crossroads. I had heard the worst and still an unknown hope of glorious salvation existed.

"Your mother met me at the door holding this month's issue of `The Immediate Family of the President for Life (Unless There's a Massive Breakthrough in Cryogenics) of the Philippines and Surrounding Suburbs, What's-his-name, House and Garden' in her hands. For many years I have only briefly skimmed this glorious periodical."

The General-to-be's father walks into the living room and returns with a copy of "The Immediate Family of the President for Life (Unless There's a Massive Breakthrough in Cryogenics) of the Philippines and Surrounding Suburbs, What's-his-name, House and Garden".

"If only I'd studied it every month, this family might not have been in the desperate situation it found itself this morning. Thank-you, my most dearest." The General-to-be's father blows a kiss to his wife. Roberto and the General-to-be exchange astonished glances.

"Your mother, my wife, the savior of us all, takes me into the parlor, sits me down in the big chair near the window, and paging through this glorious magazine, shows me the salvation of our family."

The General-to-be's father smiles, and retrieving from his wallet a four inch by four inch advertisement, hands it to the General-to-be. "My dear son, gaze upon your future."

The General-to-be takes the paper from his father's hand and stares at what will be his future.

===========

"The President for Life (Unless There's a Massive Breakthrough in Cryogenics) of the Philippines and Surrounding Suburbs, What's-his-name, announces openings in **The Palace Guard of the President for Life (Unless There's a Massive Breakthrough in Cryogenics) of the Philippines and Surrounding Suburbs, What's-his-name.** Are you **young**? Do you want to plan your **future**? Are you related by blood to **the President for Life (Unless There's a Massive Breakthrough in Cryogenics) of the Philippines and Surrounding Suburbs, What's-his-name**? Well, **Uncle What's-his-name needs you!!!** The Palace guard needs **a few good oligarchs**! Are you up to the **challenge**? Can you use both your heels? **Call today!! WE CAN FIX IT!!!**

THIS MONTHS SPECIAL: **CAPTAINCIES!!**

===========

Morning breaks over the face of the General-to-be. It's truly what he has always desired but was afraid of acknowledging to himself. Forget school. Get into the real world. The military. The General-to-be has always considered himself far too intellectual for the military. The General-to-be rises from his seat, crosses to his mother and formally kisses her. He moves to his father, they exchange military salutes. The General-to-be goes to his brother. They embrace.

"Family, I have much to do." The General-to-be clicks his heels, exits the dining room, and climbs upstairs to repack his suitcases. There will be much more room in the suitcases since he no longer needs to carry bulky and unnecessary books.

Roberto lifts his glass to toast his father. They exchange nods. "Dad, how much?"

"Roberto, let me tell you, when I figured out it would cost me less to get him a captaincy than three months expenses in the States, well, what would you have done?"

The three remaining de Laleesa's toast themselves.

Fifteen nights later - it takes this long for Señor de Laleesa's check to clear after bouncing on the first try - the General-to-be Oscar de Laleesa is installed as a captain in the Palace Guard of the President for Life (Unless There's a Massive Breakthrough in Cryogenics) of the Philippines and Surrounding Suburbs, What's-his-name, commanding thirty commoners. The rest remains Philippines and Surrounding Suburbs' history.

But we're not back to Imelda Marcos and the lost ruby slipper, or the mismatched socks of What's-his-name, quite yet. We still have to discover how General-to-be Oscar de Laleesa becomes a General.

Which takes place in, of the most unlikely of places, New York City, New York, U.S.A.P.S.. Captain Oscar's duties have expanded to now frequently include being part of Imelda's Marcos' military escort as she jets, or jetés, from fabulous world capital to fabulous world capital. As a mere captain, the General-to-be believes himself immensely fortunate to be included on this travelling team. It seems, over the course of a few months, one of the Most Esteemed and Honorable First Lady's senior maids noticed the handsome young captain and persuaded a general of the Guard that, unless she had some fun sometimes, the General would be having less and less.

And so the General-to-be is graced with a most congenial travelling companion on approximately one out of every three nights during the overseas junkets of Madame Who Might As Well Be President for Life (Unless There's a Massive Breakthrough in Cryogenics) of the Philippines and Surrounding Suburbs, What's-his-name.

While in New York City, one brisk autumn afternoon, the Captain (General-to-be), along with a general, one colonel, one major, and three other captains, is assigned as bodyguard/escort to the most funderful First Lady. This is a light detachment since no problems are anticipated owing to this particular trip being an unannounced shopping spree.

Following a short stop at one of Fifth Avenue's bookstores, where the First Lady of the Philippines and Surrounding Suburbs has a standing order for two hundred pounds of printed American culture per month, the almost Presidential party, who along with the General-to-be's military brethren consists of the Ambassador of the Philippines and Surrounding Suburbs to the United States of America and Points South, six female travelling companions of Imelda the Celebrated, and four guys who sort of hang around opening doors and carrying things, pile into five waiting stretch limousines for the block ride down Fifth Avenue to visit the shop which occasioned this junket to New York City, New York, U.S.A.P.S. in the first place.

We should know by now it's an elegant cobbler's but the problem which greets the entourage on arrival is the definite lack of awe and respect given to the Most Wondrous and Beautiful Not to Mention Spiffily Shod First Lady and Wife of the President for

Life (Unless There's a Massive Breakthrough in Cryogenics) of the Philippines and Surrounding Suburbs, What's-his-name.

Where Imelda's previous visits to this most renowned of footleries had brought not one, not two, but more than three or four footpeople/sales to wait upon her most delicious of digits, on this most ignoble of days barely one foot toady pays Her Most Awesomeladyship heed. And this buffoon, an hirsute savage of a barbarian, addresses Her Mostest in a manner to suggest Her Swellness and her gang should take a seat and he'll be with them when he finishes attending two blue haired Irish broads from Brooklyn.

Which does not sit particularly well with Seven Star General Miguel Jacksonine who must be restrained by his colonel from discharging the Army Colt the General has taken to pointing at the head of the footperson/sales.

Imelda, so to speak, takes this in stride, instantly does an about face and is ensconced anew within her limousine in under a minute.

Later the security team discovers this particular cobblery has been taken over by a group of Nipponese shoe firms, who, although the group has taken a major bath vis-à-vis investment grade shoes, was well aware of the opportunity which would eventually present itself.

Now for the good part. For today's duty the General-to-be has been fortuitously assigned to sit in Her Gloriousness's limo beside the chauffeur. A panicked American Secret Service agent, who, along with twenty other GS-15's, has been discreetly guarding Her Raveness and her entourage, comes rushing to the General-to-be's window. The Secret Service person is in aforesaid panic since previous visits to the same cobbler's emporium lasted two hours at minimum. This Secret Service supervisor has sent most of her nattily attired group to the Trump Tower for demitasse and crullers, not expecting Her Shoelessness to emerge for some time.

The General-to-be rapidly explains the diplomatic affront to the distraught agent and elaborates that there is now a three hour gap in Her Splendidness's itinerary. The Secret Service person throws up her hands in despair owing to the fact that three months of work has been wasted in planning security for this spontaneous visit. Her gesture momentarily befuddles two of her Uzi toting comrades across the street but, fortunately, there isn't what would later have been described in the news media as "TERRORIST GUNFIRE ON FIFTH AVENUE" since the Secret Service agent immediately lowers her arms as she says, "Too bad you can't take her to Thom McAn's. There's one right over there," indicating a nearby cross street.

And as the agent gesticulates, the General-to-be sees his big break and knows he will not remain a lowly General-to-be for long.

Powering down the anti-terrorist, bulletproof glass partition which separates the General-to-be from Her Backseatedness, the General-to-be explains to Her Listeningness how he is aware of a most tasteful and varied cobbler's emporium located nearby. Not only will the staff be most honored to serve Her Pumplessness, but they will extend, through the means of a courtesy card obtained by the General-to-be's brother Roberto who runs a Thom McAn their franchise in downtown Manila, a ten percent discount to Her Magicjohnsoness.

And with a mere wave of the hand, the General-to-be's fortune is made. Needless to say, the arrival of the First Lady of the Philippines and Surrounding Suburbs puts a dent in the daily routine of this particular Thom McAn's staff, but it's on this day Imelda Marcos first decides to truly set an example for the poor peasants of her country and, adding to the special ten percent discount already made available by the General-to-be, Her Discountedness hondles an extra five percent from the assistant manager trainee by agreeing to make her purchases in bulk. Her Wholesaledness places an order for fifty pounds assorted.

And so, First Lady and Wife of the President for Life (Unless There's a Massive Breakthrough in Cryogenics) of the Philippines and Surrounding Suburbs, What's-his-name, Imelda Marcos's stupendous collection of shoes begins. And through another arrangement with the assistant manager trainee, who promises to remove any telltale labeling from the fifty pounds of pumps, so no one will ever have the slightest inkling the shoes of swellness were purchased from the cobbler of most distinction, Señor Thom.

The General-to-be becomes a General the next day for saving the budget of the Philippines and Surrounding Suburbs for another year. The General-to-be, now General who is, later becomes a Knight of the Most Solemn and Tasteful Order of the Wedgie.

MANILA

And so, General Oscar de Laleesa leads the "Hanes" group on a most perilous search of the Presidential Palace. Strategically, he has broken down his group into four sections: light, dark, over the calf and argyle. Within days, the "Hanes" group discovers over two thousand orphaned socks. Fortuitously, one quarter of these, over five hundred, are under the jurisdiction of the General's "Hanes" Group. Sagely, the General submits the numerous orphaned socks he's discovered but which are outside his jurisdiction to the pyre, making the task of the other search parties somewhat more difficult.

A majority the other search groups have already fled the city and could care less about their assigned task, having secured their fortunes by waylaying the bounty of the missing "Rolex" search group.

As the Philippines and Surrounding Suburbs plunges rapidly into armed revolt, the President for Life (Unless There's a Massive Breakthrough in Cryogenics) of the Philippines and Surrounding Suburbs, What's-his-name remains unmovable without his socks. As the President for Life, etc.'s, position finally becomes untenable, he receives a telephone call from the Great Deaf Communicator who pledges not only to replace What's-his-name's socks, but promises to throw in two pairs of chaps and the trousers he wore on "King's Row" as well.

Within half an hour the helicopters are on the back lawn of the Presidential Palace. Nobody bothers telling General Oscar he should call off his search, so the General, whose main task around the palace has been keeping an up to the minute catalog on the "collection", is only capable of rescuing a mere forty percent of the "Señor Thoms". And, as logically follows, hundreds of Her Dreamboatedness's loafers are lost and scores mismatched.

MR. ROGERS' BREAKFAST

Professor Radigan can't believe his eyes. Any new domicile inevitably leads to a few semi-hallucinogenic experience but the people of this neighborhood seem a bit odder than usual in Radigan's experience. As is his wont during the academic year, he schedules any supposedly mandatory appearances at the University to the late afternoon. Radigan observes his neighborhood during the mornings.

Radigan spends the beginning of each day sitting at the console, writing a bit now and then, creating the framework for his next year's grant proposal. Every fifteen minutes or so his hands momentarily touch the keyboard and then, sitting back in his chair, he observes the neighborhood for another fifteen minutes. Now and then Radigan gets out of his chair to brew coffee.

Professor Radigan drives to the campus for a late lunch on most work days. Monday, Wednesday, and Friday afternoons are spent giving two hour talks on basic grant writing to undergraduate students. Tuesdays and Thursdays Radigan spends the afternoon drinking coffee with graduate students in the grant lab.

As the Ulysses S. Grant Professor in Social Sciences, Professor Radigan's grant lab continues to be the one "up" in Radigan's academic career. He's staffed the lab with a number of bureaucratic overachievers who do ninety-five percent of the work and a smattering of dropouts from the University of Southern California's doctoral program in mall shopping, in case Radigan should ever need to perform a minor magic trick and pull a grant rabbit out of a hat, fez, sombrero, beret, what-have-you, to assure full funding of his lab for the next decade or three.

State of the art as grant labs go, Professor Radigan's facility, located at the most ancient of commercial campuses, Northwest Brown and Williamson University, boasts up to the second direct mail computers and software. The primary research database contains the names and addresses of everyone who ever lived anywhere. An additional database contains grant proposals dating as far back as the preliminary research grant for the Trojan Horse, including Columbus's faulty proposal for reaching the mythical amusement park, India, and more recent grant requests, such as the one for a religious resort hotel, no details now available owing to the case continuing to be on appeal.

Grant writing as a doctoral and post-doctoral program is Professor Radigan's own invention. Although the process itself has been around longer then many hills, it was as a greasy, pimply undergrad when Radigan first experimented with the concept which soon became the source of his livelihood.

Simply put, grant writing equals salesmanship. You must convince the marks that even though they contribute money in a manner which might be perceived by the uninitiated few as entirely altruistic, the cash benefit they receive will rapidly surpass in value the sums they have to shell out. Many of Professor

Radigan's more successful students have gone on to rewarding careers as used car salesmen.

Shunning the private sector, owing to its lack of cash potential, Radigan decides at any early age to focus his most shining lights on the engine driving the limitless educational machine. Radigan immediately realizes higher education, as with any high performance engine, needs periodic lubrication and frequent fine tuning.

On discovering there did not exist one decent study focusing on how to get the most from the grant process itself, Radigan recruits three of his fellow graduate students, and employing primitive mass mail techniques, manages within the space of six weeks to fund the four of them for the next decade by appealing to the bureaucratic monster within each and every established foundation.

Radigan creates an endless, indecipherable loop, guaranteeing for both himself and numerous administrators lifetime employment with cradle to grave job security.

What, Radigan posits to the various fund administrators, can be considered the justification of, and purpose for, the present grant system? It's a simple enough question but as he roughly formulates it, Radigan realizes he's fashioned the ultimate hook.

By attempting a study on the present day grant system, Radigan taps into an endless stream of meaningless data which eventually will be elevated into academic research owing to the people involved with the origin of the data as much as anything else.

It works like this. A study is proposed. The study goes into great depth detailing the necessity for the grant administrator's job. If the position is proved necessary, how can it be improved? Should there be personnel changes? Should budgets be cut? On the other hand, what if the present grant system has outlived its usefulness? What should the alternatives look like? Is there a need for such a process at all? What should be done with the newly unemployed "grant administrators"?

Bingo!

Radigan knew he'd have them running in fear for their careers for decades. As "grant administrators", Radigan's correspondents knew one thing for a certainty, it wasn't long ago in the past when they didn't have beneficent titles like "grant administrators". Back then they were simply called "clerks".

Over the course of generations, one of their fellow "clerks" managed to con some dotty fifth generation heir to another great booze fortune into addressing this upscale bureaucrat as "grant administrator". The title stuck since foundations and charitable trusts exist mainly to blow the horns of their most esteemed and honorable benefactors. Having a group of "clerks" entitled "grant administrators" leads to the aggrandizement not only of the upgraded "clerks", but the foundation itself, and therefore to the various mucky mucks who decrease their liability by tossing a few charitable bucks by way of their local politicians or IRS men.

What could be more aggrandizing than if the entire field were represented by a university discipline created to study the field? Obviously, this would raise the realm of respect for grant review to a level equal with that of history and mathematics. Some of those who immediately jumped on Radigan's concept were historians and mathematicians who were only too aware to whom they had to suck up each and every year in order to keep their present research afloat.

Professor Radigan immediately latched on to every iota of proffered help from these established academics. They immediately appreciate the concept that by being part of Radigan's grant review review procedure, they can achieve some small bit of leverage over the low level bureaucrats who wield far too much control over their academic careers.

With his numerous co-conspirators lined up, Radigan creates, within the space of a few shortish years, the Institute of Grant Procedures, whose sole purpose becomes reviewing the process by which Radigan amasses his fortune.

Professor Radigan often likens his profession to being paid for every drop of rain which falls because he can explain why rain falls from the sky. It is good.

However, Radigan doesn't make the lion's share of his living by mere academic research. His far more lucrative side line consists of hiring out as a consultant for fellow academic grant writers.

A frustrated scholar getting nowhere with the grant procedure, approaches Professor Radigan. Radigan customizes another of his standardized grant applications, including a line item for Radigan's consultation fee.

Bingo!

Any self-respecting "grant administrator" recognizes Radigan's standard form and immediately scans the application to locate Radigan's fee. By adjusting the percentage of the grant represented by this line item, the "grant administrator" can tell how much weight Radigan puts behind the project, this being the sole criterion by which the "grant administrator" establishes the total grant amount.

History has forever been an odd and entertaining field of discipline. You endeavor to uncover what were the realities of a given period, then you attempt to create an unassailable theory which explains the facts you have unearthed.

Professor Radigan's history reveals him to be a man solely dedicated to the advancement of a new academic field of inquiry as well as his own career, not necessarily in that order, and not necessarily separable. For the first fifteen years of his academic career, Radigan dedicates himself solely to the success of the program he's invented, and when he finally came up for air, Professor Radigan took an inordinately large gulp.

On awakening from his deep academic sleep, Radigan realizes he's become an anachronism in his own time. Bringing his shirts to the commercial laundry as he's done every Saturday for the past decade, he is brought up short when the laundryman behind the counter shakes his head "no" and shoves the pile of button-downs back to the startled professor.

"No more."

Radigan becomes confused. "Do I owe anything on my bill?" This is the only possible reason Radigan can imagine for such rude and uncustomary behavior.

"Shirts no good. Look." And the laundryman behind the counter takes one of seven identical white oxford cloth dress shirts into his hands and holds the point of its button-down collar in his right hand then uses his left to snatch the other point while snapping the collar, which immediately separates in a manner similar to the special effects used for Moses crossing the Red Sea.

"Shirts won't live past machine."

Which makes sense to Radigan. He picks up one of the remaining shirts and conducts the same experiment, producing a similar bi-blousal result.

The laundryman behind the counter grins. "Buy new shirts. Look sharp. Feel sharp." With this the laundryman gathers the shirts together and drops them into a bin next to him which isn't the bin into which the man behind the counter usually drops

Radigan's weekly consignment of white, oxford cloth, button-down shirts.

"Right." Radigan at long last awakens from his dream of grants within grants within grants. Although for years he's been receiving extremely healthy checks every two weeks or so, Radigan routinely deposits them into his savings account at the University credit union. He's lived in University housing, it seems, forever. Most of his meals are charged to his department, picked up by "grant administrators", or handled by those poor academics who pay dearly for having Radigan to consult. His expenses have remained minimal.

Radigan realizes he's stagnated. He vaguely remembers the joy he experienced as an undergraduate, standing in front of a mirror and checking himself out, adjusting his tie, removing lint from his suit, before a big date.

A date. Radigan vaguely remembers the last one he had. For too long a time he has sublimated everything to his grant goals.

Radigan considers himself a personable enough guy. Now and then he's been called good-looking. But he has become a driven man, focused on but one objective and this one objective has obscured the other facets of his life.

Leaving the commercial laundry, Professor Radigan makes the short drive back to the University apartment he's occupied for over ten years. Entering his flat, Radigan passes the main room; living area, kitchen, bay windows; and opens the door to the clothes closet in his bedroom. Sliding open the door, Radigan greets what must have been considered the height of undergraduate elegance fifteen years back. He takes the blue blazer he's worn to every business meeting he's ever attended from its hanger. Radigan always wore the blazer with one of the dear, departed, white, oxford cloth, button-down shirts. He takes the jacket by the collar and performs the test previously performed by the laundryman behind the counter at the dry cleaners. Radigan feels great relief as the jacket doesn't vaporize in the same manner as the shirts.

Then Professor Radigan realizes that with a heavier fabric like the blazer's, perhaps he should apply a bit more force. He does, and the jacket is suddenly suitable exclusively for slot machines.

All this depresses Radigan. Not that he has an extensive wardrobe, but as he tests the strength of his clothes, the vast majority fail the test.

After a half-hour, Professor Radigan is left with a closet in which hangs one down parka and a University sweatshirt Radigan was given two years ago by a grateful, soon to become well endowed, graduate student. Strewn about the floor are the remains of pods which once veiled his life.

Radigan reminds himself of a butterfly. Shoveling the rags into a plastic garbage bag, Radigan adds the contents of his underwear drawer, most of his shoes and sneakers, a half dozen ties, and fifteen, white, crew necked undershirts, most of which are boldly illuminated by yellow sweat circles about the armpits.

Radigan feels a weight lifted from his torso. Entering the kitchenette, Radigan rummages through a drawer where he tosses everything he can't figure out where else to toss. The junk drawer.

Over the years, Radigan periodically received in the mail, credit cards of ever imaginable size, shape, payment plan and plastic fabrication. Since the only need for a credit card Radigan, until today, could imagine was buying gas for his car, he'd flung them into this junk drawer. After all, his department picked up expenses on the car. Professor Radigan now feels a need for plastic in his own name.

Radigan finds three bank cards containing valid expiration dates, signs the backs and is on his way.

Driving into the center of town Professor Radigan realizes this journey will be different. For years, whenever he needed replenishment of his basic supplies, a new pair of jeans, some sneakers, a pair of BVD's, the most he had to do was stroll into the village and drop into the army-navy store. His sizes never changed and neither did the army-navy store's stock. It worked perfectly.

As Radigan stares at the site of his beloved provisioner, he feels the passage of years heavily. Where once stood Radigan's shrine to functional fashion, now reigns a mini-mall. Pulling into the parking lot, Radigan decides to question the owner of what appears to be a jeans' store as to the location of his former haberdasher.

Inside, Radigan is bombarded with options and variations of geometric proportions. He never had any choice in the army-navy store. The owners stocked two styles of jeans, overalls and not overalls. The Professor consistently chose the not overalls.

Radigan stands in amazement. There are literally hundreds of jean choices arrayed before him. A thirtysomethingish Filipino man approaches.

B.H.B.S.

The compact human entity likes what she sees. There are thirty pieces of matching alligator skin luggage arrayed in a row on the sidewalk in front of her. The compact human entity took the job as assistant to the door man of this three star Beverly Hills hotel when her young man abruptly disappeared from this same hotel, leaving the compact human entity without any of the purchases she'd made using the young man's credit cards, as well as a sizable bill the manager demanded be paid.

Faced with a choice between prosecution and gradually working off her bill as assistant to the door man, the compact human entity opts for the entry level/career potential job.

WITHDRAWAL

What we're talking about here is withdrawal. And I'm not talking about taking it from a bank. Take Imelda Marcos, for example. There she was, First Lady of the Philippines and Surrounding Suburbs. Suddenly she's got nothing. Imagine the withdrawal such a termagant as she went through. It has to be worse than jail. She was addicted to so much. Power. Adulation. Mobility. Noblesse oblige. I'm not even talking about drugs. Who can say what this weird sister pumped into her body each and every day? Maybe she didn't. Maybe the trappings of her office were enough for her to get off. Doubt it. Especially when she knew the end was coming. And boy, she must have seen it from way off.

Addiction. Addiction even to being nice. Addiction to anything. Addiction to not being addicted. Randomness. It's white nine times out of ten. Black one out of twenty. Green one out of forty. And anything goes the rest of the time. Maybe a plaid. Possibly a polyhedral skyscraper. Sometimes a pet dog lost in the woods.

Non-addiction. The ability to do anything. At any time. For no reason discernible to anyone. Forget Freud, Jung, and those folks. Jimmy the Greek can't make the odds. Any psychics worth their salt shakers can't see past their noses on this one. Arthur C. Clarke folds his hand.

SIMPERING SALESMEN

She's hanging around a hotel room not in a tropical paradise. She's not building Holiday Inns in the middle of another godforsaken jungle. She's not throwing parties for simpering salesmen masquerading as the diplomatic corps. She's bored.

Imelda Marcos knows what she needs to know to survive on her own in the big world out there. After all, she'd taken foolish What's-his-name and brought him from being a two-bit junk salesman to the Presidential Palace and What's-his-name wouldn't know a Ford Bronco from a heifer.

Imelda Marcos has been through tough times before. During the Nipponese occupation, she'd barely been able to eke out a living selling ganjah to the evil sons of the Rising Sun, so she worked part-time at "Ronrico's Travelling Wonder Bar", located on the back of an old farm wagon, and toured hordes of troop camps offering a variety of delights from saki to a Filipino version of the traditional tea ceremony. Imelda Marcos never was able to master Nipponese, the haiku, or koto, so she mainly worked behind the portable bar and sometimes underneath the wagon if cash flow became a pressing problem.

The future Mr. and Mrs. President for Life (Unless There's a Massive Breakthrough in Cryogenics) of the Philippines and Surrounding Suburbs, What's-his-name met one historic evening when What's-his-name and a crew of his co-workers came down from the hills to pay their monthly tribute to the Nipponese officer in charge of the camp for their district. "Ronrico's Travelling Wonder Bar" happened to be playing there at the time. In order for his operation to survive, leveling the "patriotic tax" on the usual peasants, What's-his-name was forced to share a lion's portion of his take with the Nipponese occupiers.

This wasn't anything remotely resembling any kind of original scam. The Nipponese picked it up from the Russian First Directorate who'd picked it up from every occupying force preceding them.

The occupiers knew they hadn't enough troops to maintain in depth control over the Philippines and Surrounding Suburbs. With limited manpower available, the Nipponese needed to recruit local talent for day-to-day housekeeping. Local operatives were necessary to keep the civilian population in a state of relative panic and the occupiers found it convenient to employ folks already trained in the fear and loathing department. The neighborhood banditos fit the job description.

One day the occupiers brought a few of the indigenous bandit chiefs in for an intimate little chitchat. The chiefs are given the option of working for the great flag of the Semi-Rising Sun or digging ditches as foundations for their own permanent underground time share condominiums. The chief banditos make the mature decision to continue with their business as usual and sign on as employees of the occupying forces.

So, What's-his-name and the other bandit chiefs become the Resistance Army of the Philippines and Surrounding Suburbs. They sow terror in the villages, collect taxes for the great Resistance Army of the Philippines and Surrounding Suburbs, and shortchange the Nipponese as much as possible. The occupiers, of course, execute a few banditos now and then to remind the Great Resistance Army of the Philippines and Surrounding Suburbs that the Great Army of the Semi-Rising Sun is trying hard to keep the banditos honest. The occupiers operate similarly to governments everywhere.

The Nipponese insist if the bandito armies of resistance ever meet any legitimate resistance fighters, the legitimate resistance fighters be turned over to them. The banditos, of course, oblige. Most of the time. The bandito chiefs know every new and improved government must eventually pass to another new and improved government and they endeavor to keep all six sides (including the crusts) of their bread well buttered.

As often happens during the monthly accounting missions, one of the Nipponese muckworms, Colonel Toewhat, deigned to address What's-his-name and his loyal followers. The banditos considered these regular indoctrination sessions simply another price they had to pay for their lucrative franchises.

"Fellow loyal followers of the great Empire of the Semi-Rising Sun. The Philippines and Surrounding Suburbs are ours for the taking. We control the islands, and the people. Ours is the destiny which will bring our great nation and ourselves to the manifest destiny we so richly deserve.

"Our neat and swell Emperor has reminded us time and again exactly what our future will entail. In the years to come our great nation of the Semi-Rising Sun will stretch from semi-rising sun to semi-rising sunset.

"The arms of the Emperor will reach into every home. The Emperor's arms attached by cords of strength will manipulate all people everywhere and the people will be told exactly how they must behave in order to serve the great empire of the Semi-Rising Sun. Through this entry into the homes of all peoples the Emperor will be known as He transmits His thoughts to all His subjects.

Colonel Toewhat pauses in his discourse. "The Emperor knows none of His great goals will be easy to accomplish. Already He is training cadres of corporate commandos who will bring to fruition his dreams of the one true Imperial Corporation once our military missions have accomplished their tasks." Concluding his speech Colonel Toewhat turns his back to his audience by spinning on his heels while at the same time managing to perform one of the newer dance steps popular back home the last time he had some leave. He knew the performance could not be appreciated by his audience of barbarians but Colonel Toewhat liked to stay in practice. What's-his-name and his band of merry men remain suitably unimpressed.

Coming down to the bar following Colonel Toewhat's speech and after paying the monthly tax on the tax, What's-his-name stops by "Ronrico's Travelling Wonder Bar" with a few of the boys and discovers Imelda deftly tending bar. Imelda has no idea what these second-rate yahoos have in mind and keeps her mouth shut as the six roughnecks settle themselves onto the portable barstools of the portable bar.

As they settle in, the boys look to What's-his-name to make the first move. What's-his-name remains silent in his seat as he takes in Imelda, who just so happens to be the first non-native woman he's seen in the past month.

Imelda stands in silence.

"Boys, she may not be the prettiest, but at least she knows when to keep her mouth shut."

And some say this was the biggest mistake What's-his-name made over the course of his entire career.

After six or seven of Imelda's famous sterno and pineapple punches, What's-his-name motions his lieutenant and the supposedly silent Imelda is rapidly trussed up, stuffed into a canvas sack and carried off on the shoulders of the largest of What's-his-name's men.

Some say this was the last time Imelda ever kept her thoughts to herself.

Those were tough days for Imelda. After being carried off into the hills and making the acquaintance of the members of What's-his-name's band of dedicated resistance tax collectors, Imelda became irreplaceable to the group, owing to her knowledge of physical activities not previously known in these parts of the islands. After exhausting the advantages to be gleamed from his underlings, Imelda set her cap on the legendary resistance fighter himself, What's-his-name and the rest remains indelibly inscribed in the history of the Philippines and Surrounding Suburbs.

But now things have changed. Imelda sits looking into her makeup mirror reassuring herself the four hours of intense effort by her three makeup women is holding up.

Imelda examines her face softly singing a song to herself. It's the old song she sang while holding court for the members of What's-his-name's resistance group.

It's a pretty song relating the tale of a young woman from the countryside who survives by selling native produce by the seashore. She eventually meets a band of heroic resistance fighters and she later becomes queen of the islands. It's a song guaranteed to lift Imelda's spirits.

With a knock on the door, the stage manager enters Imelda's dressing room and informs the former first lady of the Philippines and Surrounding Suburbs it's five minutes to air.

On the air again. Imelda Marcos's face and voice flying through the sky as if by magic. No longer is she the constant voice to millions of her people. No longer do millions tremble in fear and awe, analyzing her every syllable, each subtle movement of her butterfly like hands. This will be different. Imelda Marcos will persevere.

Another knock on the door.

Two minutes.

-This will be my start! Those little people so jealous of my beauty, my grace, my intelligence, my power, my husband, What's-his-name, my angelic singing voice, my nails, my hair, my dresses, my shoes, my hairstyle, my carriage. They cannot stand being such insignificant people, peasants, in my presence.

-When did they start their insidious plots? Hadn't I brought them from the gutter into the most gracious and beautiful palace in the world? I allowed them to step inside the wonder of it all and they repay me by stabbing What's-his-name and myself in the back and sending us both into exile.

-They shall pay. This will only be the start. From this small broadcast shall I begin to rebuild the glory which was once the Philippines and Surrounding Suburbs. Imelda Marcos shall return!-

One minute.

Imelda rechecks her makeup. Perfect. Her hairdresser deserted her, starting her own shop in Beverly Hills and the local woman took twice as long to produce a result which still needs Imelda's own refined hand to complete her crowning glory.

Almost perfect. It will have to do. She must not worry. This will be more majesty than her audience will have seen in their entire life. Not since the second inauguration of her most radiant highness, Nancy Reagan, has the world beheld such glory.

Almost time. Imelda Marcos lifts herself from her seat and rising to her full four feet eleven inches of imperial majesty, struts from her dressing room to meet, once again, her date with destiny, her second coming, her ascent from the ashes like the phoenix of ancient myth, her chance to fully reestablish her credit line at the proper shop, a job of her own, her new career, I am womanish watch me now. She's psyched. She's ready. She's hot. She's new. She's the role model for the nineties. She's Imelda.

"Ladies and Gentlemen." The staff announcer addresses the audience within the cable television studio and the infinitely larger audience of their cable broadcast area. "Ladies and Gentlemen, this is almost too fantastic a task for me to handle. Ladies and gentlemen, it's with immense pleasure we welcome you today to the most historic broadcast in television history.

"It's with immense pleasure that the management and staff bring you the most lovely, the most charming, the most witty, the best dressed, the most talented, the totally delightful, former First Lady of the Philippines and Surrounding Suburbs, her hostess avec the extreme mostest, the new shining star of "MIDDAY ALBANY", **Imelda Marcos!!!**

And with thunderous applause only an audience of ninety people can bestow upon one such as herself, Imelda enters from behind a downstage curtain, bows to both the home and live audience, finds her mark, and smiling her most regal of smiles, waits for the tape to cue up then launches into her signature rendition of "I Am Woman".

The audience listens in appreciative amazement as the words to a song which became totally passé a mere decade past is delivered in a heavily accented country and western style best described as an inept attempt at Pan Pacific Low Camp.

As Imelda wraps up her song, watching the faces of her absolutely stunned audience and completely misinterpreting the origin of their shock, she takes her bows and soaks in the thunderous ovation prompted by every red, flashing, applause sign the studio has to offer. The producers, as usual staying a step ahead of the talent, installed an extra fifteen applause signs in honor of Imelda's debut on local Albany cable television, bringing the total number to twenty-nine.

This isn't an audience shanghaied from the usual passers-bys. This is an invited audience who over the years has shown the most enthusiasm when prompted by these low tech, low voltage show business cattle prods. The producers leave nothing to chance. After a month on local the producers expect to syndicate the show on national cable. This is the beginning. The producers' intend to become multi-millionaires before they achieve the age of twenty-seven.

Elated by the response of these loving American fans, Imelda remains blissfully unaware most of this choice audience has been recruited from local rest homes and halfway houses. The audience remains aware of the ever present production assistants charting them according to their visible enthusiasm. The audience was well instructed before the beginning of the show that those who are the most enthusiastic in their response will be given various fabulous prizes as well as a hot catered lunch and those who fail to make the cut will be sent home with a couple of bologna sandwiches in brown paper bags. The audience is appropriately enthusiastic.

"Thank-you. Thank-you, each and every one of you, so very, very much. I love all of you with all my heart." And as the three piece, mostly synthesized, studio band launches into the "MIDDAY ALBANY" theme, loosely based on the Philippines and Surrounding Suburbs national anthem, Imelda makes her way back to the living room style chair which will serve as her throne during the run of the show. "MIDDAY ALBANY"'s set designer has created a masterpiece of local midday news/entertainment/talk show design. Imelda is surrounded by the ghost of a "HOUSE AND GARDEN" idea of a typical New England style family room. There is, of course, no dust on the lamp shades.

"Thank-you so very, very much." Imelda now takes command of the set projecting the personality which held an entire nation hostage for many years. "Since this is our first show, I want to introduce you to my co-host. This is a person all of you must know from the wonderful publicity she's received in the last few weeks. Let's have a nice, warm, Albany welcome for **THE COMPACT HUMAN ENTITY!!!**"

And with such a complimentary introduction, Imelda stands, applauds, and turns to see the compact human entity enter from stage right. The compact human entity wears the most traditional Swiss dress seen since the precisely on schedule showing of "Heidi" was responsible for the death of two dozen network executives by irate American football fans.

The host and co-host of "MIDDAY ALBANY" embrace as the audience pays the cost of their lunch enthusiastically. Imelda and the compact human entity appear as if they haven't seen each other in over a decade and both had assumed the other killed, raped, and kidnapped by bands of marauding maniacs who first plucked out their fingernails and then began to critique the way they dressed with a violence only seen in "W" on an extremely bad day.

As the weep fest subsides the compact human entity does a half turn reminiscent of the woman with the unlimited wardrobe who flips cards even though it's obvious the cards could easily flip themselves. The studio audience again enthusiastically applauds and some members of the audience, along with most of the stage crew who know for certain which way is up, sound a few wolf whistles to which the compact human entity responds with what looks like a genuine blush but actually is an emulation the compact human entity learned during one of her first intense training sessions with the former first lady of the Philippines and Surrounding Suburbs.

As the ovation from the audience recedes to a mere roar, the two hosts seat themselves, facing one another, holding hands. A member of the crew begins the "Ooohs" and "Aaahs" and the underfed peanut gallery picks up the Hallmarkish sentiment.

Imelda reads the sentiment permeating the studio, she racks her brain for a moment and comes up with the appropriate tune. The former first lady of the Philippines and Surrounding Suburbs gives a silent cue to the bandleader and launches into a torpid rendition of "Feelings", a showstopper Imelda would use repeatedly whenever one of her mass rallies began to flag. Holding back a few beats, the compact human entity joins in.

The two women sing directly to each other and at a cue from the director relayed by the stage manager to the co-hosts, Imelda and the compact human entity turn to the audience and continue with the second verse of the song in what might be considered a spontaneous attempt at harmony which fails bravely, but in reality is a horrible attempt at harmony practiced an hour a day over the past two weeks.

As the orchestra leader brings the tune to a triumphant conclusion, the two women embrace for the umpteenth time since the song began, and the director signals one of his technicians as well as the stage manager. "MIDDAY ALBANY" cuts for commercial.

Somewhere in a tropical jungle.
Night.

C.U.	Parrot sitting on branch of broad-leaved tree. Parrot squawks, flies away in reaction to sound of branches being broken underfoot.
C.U.	Imelda Marcos, Former First Lady of the Philippines and Surrounding Suburbs, turns her head to the left, reacts in fear to what she sees.
Reveal	Imelda running through jungle, pushing branches out of the way. One branch scrapes her face causing slight scratch on direct center of left cheek bone.
P.O.V.	Pursuers watch Imelda, in Clarence of Beverly Hills sarong, make her way through undergrowth.
Wide	Pursuers, three young men, handsome, heavily armed, draped in Banana Republic camouflage green guerilla suits. They carry machetes and proceed through jungle at much quicker pace than Imelda. They shout and point to their quarry.
Wide	Imelda arrives at shore of raging river. Crocodile (alligator if cheaper) prowls nearby shore. (Stock footage. Be careful about match. We can do lab work on this one.)
C.U.	Imelda realizes her escape route is blocked. Brief look of panic flashes across her face.
Med.	Former First Lady of the Philippines and Surrounding Suburbs remembers who she is,

taking deep breath decides to confront pursuers and regally stand her ground.

Wide   Guerrillas sight their target, raising weapons they decrease pace and begin slow stalk towards Imelda.

Wide   Imelda Marcos former First Lady of the Philippines and Surrounding Suburbs stands with river at her back, majestically facing opponents.

Med.   Imelda dabs back of her neck with "*Imelda, the Perfume*", **LABEL FACING CAMERA**

C.U.   Lead guerilla sniffs air. Suspicion then pleasure register on his face.

Med.   Guerilla #2 sniffs air then straightens out his uniform and runs hand through hair in attempt to improve appearance.

Med.   Guerilla #3 stares in direction of Imelda Marcos, throws rifle and machete to ground, begins trance like walk to Imelda.

Long   The three guerrillas surround Imelda. Guerrilla #1 lies on back gazing into Imelda's face. Guerilla #2 kneels on right leg offering Imelda flower. Guerilla #3 stands guard behind Imelda scanning area making sure nothing will approach his queen unnoticed.

Graph   "*IMELDA, THE PERFUME*. Rule your world." Leave bottom line open for local co-sponsor. I.E., in small print. "Available now at your local K-mart and other fine perfumers."

Following a commercial for Farmer Fred's feedlot, the home audience views the image of Imelda and the compact human entity standing in the kitchen set, surrounding a pedestal table covered with innumerable utensils.

"Thankyouallsoverymuch!   Thankyouthankyouthankyou!" During the break Imelda managed to change gowns and tiaras. She now appears wearing the latest in haute cuisine aprons draped about her torso. The compact human entity has shifted into a more demure shift.

"Today, the compact human entity and I are very proud to have as our guest that most eminent of authors, the fearless Rap novelist, the most sought after guest for any talk show in the country, Salaam Rush D! Salaam Rush D is here today, not to talk about anything as boring as the much publicized to-do over his latest book, "The Diabolic Cow", but to show us how to make one of his favorite recipes, coq au vin. Ladies and gentlemen, dear friends, Salaam Rush D!"

MORE TRUCKS

Eventually Big Aloysius decides that if he can't find Little Aloysius then it's time for Little Aloysius to find him.

For two months Big Aloysius cruised the country with the truck driver, most of the time staring from the passenger window feverishly hoping to spot Little Aloysius. After a few weeks of this futile effort, the driver decides it's time for a change. He's known his share of peculiar people in his time, and he expected Big Aloysius to emerge from his funk after a few thousand miles. The truck driver isn't easily put off by anyone's silence and odd behavior, but Big Aloysius finally got to him.

"Hey, big buddy, don't you think you should give it a rest?"

The tone of the truck driver's voice gets Big Aloysius's attention.

Big Aloysius never means to be unsociable. Far from it. Big Aloysius considers himself the most congenial of people. Unfortunately for Big Aloysius, the majority of people he's encountered during his adult life don't share this belief.

Big Aloysius started being called Big Aloysius early in life. At birth. His mother insisted "Big Aloysius" be printed on the certificate. It was her last request. Weighing in at a mere twenty-three pounds, ten ounces, Big Aloysius's mom wanted the world to know why she wasn't going to be around as her son grew into what she accurately assumed would be an ample adulthood.

Raised as an only child by a father who was away much of the time gathering the food needed to fuel the child's massive machine, Big Aloysius, as a charming toddler a hair under five feet tall, revealed the fallacy in attempting to childproof anything.

Through grade school, Big Aloysius proves anything but adaptable to his surroundings. His schoolmates and teachers prove unable to accommodate his inordinate height and girth. A few coaches try utilizing his mighty size but height and girth don't necessarily go hand in paw with speed, strength or agility.

With every eye turning to him whenever he enters a room, Big Aloysius gradually withdraws into himself. There are no other children like him and no field of endeavor appears capable of handling his presence.

Alone. Big and alone. Massive and alone. Huge and alone. Monstrous and alone.

Big Aloysius does not fit in with his surroundings. Literally. In his first days of elementary school, finding a seat for Big Aloysius drives the administration of the institution beyond the brink of insanity. There is no chance Big Aloysius, as a five foot seven inch, two hundred pound first grader, will fit into any available desk. The desks were designed for ordinary children, four foot tall wonders of cheer and enthusiasm. They were not designed for Big Aloysius. He becomes moody and resigned.

And so it went through the days of his abbreviated academic career. Big Aloysius spends most of his school days gazing out classroom windows. This is facilitated by his placement on the most convenient windowsill in every class he attends. Windowsills are the only spots roomy enough for Big Aloysius to comfortably perch himself.

Big Aloysius learns early that even if his classmates hate him and tease him horribly, he cannot fight back. After hospitalizing a fellow third grader, Big Aloysius's father has Big Aloysius promise never again to use his fists in anger. This is fine with Big Aloysius.

As years pass, Big Aloysius discovers his only friends to be the dogs his father gives him as pets. They accept him without reservation. The dogs have no way of judging Big Aloysius's size against other men. Big Aloysius feeds them. They love Big Aloysius.

And so it went until one day, at age fifteen, a strapping seven foot three, two hundred and eighty-seven pounds and still growing, Big Aloysius decides nothing in present day architecture can hold him. Taking his present hound, Little Aloysius, along, Big Aloysius heads into the woods, leaving a note for his father who now has enough groceries for a month, rather than a short week.

As Big Aloysius ponders the history he's been recalling, the truck driver downshifts and pulls into one of the many roadside stops designed for massive interstate tractor trailers like his.

The truck driver hands the keys to Big Aloysius and elaborates on how the deal works.

"Listen careful now, big buddy. You've watched me long enough. I'm sure you know how to drive this rig. I've told you what you need to know about maintenance. You know the stops you've got to make. Here's the license. Here's the route book. Here's the papers. You pick me up, right here, in one month. Happy motoring!"

This seems like a fine deal to Big Aloysius. Big Aloysius, his silence notwithstanding, isn't a fool. As his size increased so had Big Aloysius's intelligence. With no friends, Big Aloysius found books to be non-aggressive companions. Finishing high school early, his premature departure having more to do with his teachers wanting Big Aloysius's mass out of their class than with anything else, Big Aloysius felt adequately prepared to deal with the outside world, at least as a theoretical concept. The woods in which he lives don't lend themselves to intense socializing.

Big Aloysius knows what he must do to find Little Aloysius. From watching the television show, "MIDDAY ALBANY!" he'd identified with the images he viewed on the screen. Big Aloysius can't place exactly where these feelings of familiarity begin or end, so it isn't until near the end of the show everything seemed to click into place.

Months before Big Aloysius met the driver while searching for Little Aloysius, a day came when Big Aloysius found himself in a city where the climate did not suit his clothes. He'd been on one of his many searches for Little Aloysius and this time the two of them eventually caught up with one another in a town almost a continent away from their home woods. The reunion was a joyous event in Big Aloysius's memory and the time the two companions spent in that city and most of the journey home was overshadowed in Big Aloysius's memory by the satisfaction of reunion of man with beast.

Still, Big Aloysius remembers some of the events which occurred while he was in the hot, dry city.

Big Aloysius remembers when he finally spotted Little Aloysius on the opposite side of the street. There are a great number of automobiles hurtling about and immediately Big Aloysius becomes concerned over the safety of his small friend with so many pieces of high powered aluminum darting about the street. Big Aloysius comes close to jumping into the middle of the traffic but restrains himself on realizing Little Aloysius has yet to discover his presence and is simply hanging around shop windows looking in to see if there is anything which might interest your average oversized hound.

REAL POOP

It's tough being a dog. You might imagine canines have it made in the shade. Let me tell you they don't. It's been years since I bothered putting my thoughts into words and over these years the amount of insensitivity I've witnessed which mankind heaps on me and those like me could fill enough volumes to masquerade as an encyclopedia.

-Don't get me wrong. I'm not complaining here. If I didn't like the life I'm living I could change it in a minute. The problem is so many of my peers have forgotten how to better their lives. They accept behavior I wouldn't even tolerate on one of my good days. Which are becoming fewer and fewer the more I get on in life.

-Let's see, where to begin.

-I'll skip most of the early chapters since unless the kennel caught fire on the day you were born the initial details of any hound's life are remarkably similar. I'm talking about those of us who managed to adapt enough so they are considered by humans as being "domesticated".

-"Domesticated". Right.

-I'll get back to this particular bone of contention later.

-Anyhow, early on I was separated from the rest of the geeks in my litter and my mom, and taken away to an eminently forgettable three bedroom split level in the suburbs. The place was a dump but what did I know then?

-The kid is a geek. Spotted this right off and even though we've known each other for years, I still find myself apologizing to no one in particular for his goofiness.

-Not that I didn't enjoy the woods. Hell, it's the smartest move he ever made. Only took me a couple of years to get him to make the move. We'd run around doing a whole lot of nothing for days at a time. When the time came when the kid thought he should be going home, I always tried to get him to stick around a bit longer. Hell, if you were me, where would you prefer to hang out, in a woods with a couple of thousand trees and as much the fresh air you can breathe, or some tinkertoy split level where they recirculate the air to heat it or cool it and the only scent you can distinguish occurs when the old man has to spray the bathroom to keep the place partially civilized.

-So we hit the woods and, hey, I admit it, I had a good time for a while. The kid made himself some sort of klutzoid hut for himself and eventually built a useable lean-to for me. We'd run around looking for stuff to eat and when I treed a rabbit or a squirrel, the kid did the dirty work. Hell, he had to be good for something.

-The motorcycles were my idea. I mean, how long could you handle it if the only thing you ever did consisted of running around some woods twenty-four hours a day with the same goofball kid? Not long, I'll tell you right off.

-So I got a little spoiled over the years. Do you have any idea what they put in cans of so called "dog food"? Let me tell you, they're not as lousy as you think. Actually, they're it's pretty darn good. Talk about a competitive business. How do you think it is these companies get the average pet owner to shell out hard earned money for what the owner thinks are table scraps? Product. Product sells every time.

-Have you ever tasted undercooked squirrel? Undercooked rabbit isn't exactly one of my fave raves either. Eventually it became pretty tough remembering the sound of my beloved can opener. I still salivate when I think about it. So what if it doesn't have the romance of an open camp fire, clean air and Spring fresh trees. We're talking food here. This isn't a subject I take lightly. Studies have shown food, the gathering and consuming of food, occupies over fifty percent of non-sleeping hours for your average canine. We're discussing serious business here.

-So the kid thought I'd stay with him and be his friend forever. Hey, they've been thinking the same thing for thousands of years. Man's best friend. Right. Run around for hours without stopping, your tongue hanging out and everybody thinks you're another dumb hound just like every other dumb hound. Hey, I'm not saying some pooches haven't become as daffy as the British royal family from generations of inbreeding, but they're the "purebreds". Monty Python would reunite if they knew the skinny on that one.

-What are you talking about? You think because you call dogs "Fido" we're supposed to hang around some blockhead our entire life? Listen, you start talking pragmatists, you start talking canines.

-I don't know how he found me. You'd think my going to California would be sufficient to discourage him. It wasn't. Every week or so you hear stories about dogs finding their way across the country to locate their original "masters". Let me tell you, if they could have made it where they were, they'd never start any return cross-country hikes.

-Sure, you see these dumb mutts on the tube, scarred and mangy, drooling over some fool when they get back from their cross-country junkets after being abandoned in Yellowstone Park and hiking two thousand or so miles only to return to glorious Passaic, New Jersey. Those dumb mutts never get it into their heads that their "master" abandoned them intentionally. They do a two year cross multi-state tour to return to the same jerk who deserted them to start with. Humans have the same problem with abusive behavior. The victim keeps coming back for more.

-Let's face it, after so much walking and fending for itself, what's the end result? The "owner" and the mutt get their picture in the local paper. How does this help the mutt who's dumb enough to make the return trip? Not at all. Maybe he gets a few extra strokes from overly perfumed ladies, maybe an extra bone or real canned from the "master" while the publicity stays hot. Then what?

-After a couple of weeks the "master" comes down from the high of having his picture in the paper with the mutt. The extra bones begin to disappear. The pooch finds himself left alone for longer and longer periods of time. If the hound makes a small mistake here or there, the punishment becomes extraordinarily harsh in relation to the offense. Pretty soon old routines reestablish themselves. Pretty soon the abandoned hound is having doubts whether the sacrifices he's made to reunite himself with the "master" are worth it. Pretty soon the dumb canine is damn well sure he's made a big mistake.

-Then what happens? Obviously the mutt wasn't too bright from the get go. If he'd a couple more points of I.Q., he'd have realized when he was abandoned in Yellowstone, or wherever, before he began his lengthy cross country trek, that what he was returning to really wasn't worth the effort. Pretty soon the "master" realizes not only doesn't he enjoy having the pooch around, the pooch costs him money. To the "master" the mutt does only two things: the first is, the mutt eats; the second being a direct result of the first.

-The "master" starts withholding the one thing which should guarantee fidelity from any hound, be it clever or moronic. The food starts appearing at erratic intervals. This can go on for some weeks. Then the food stops altogether. The pooch is puzzled.

-Let me tell you something about the canine species. We don't have the greatest understanding of what people consider "time". People wear wristwatches, we don't. We've been sitting here having this chat for some time. How long would you say?

"Oh, about forty-five minutes."

-Right. For me that forty-five minutes could have been two or three human hours. Possibly nine or ten. Or it might have been matter of minutes. People can appreciate a day chopped into infinite fragments. For a dog, we only appreciate a sunrise or sunset. We can remember events which took place within a certain day but we can't distinguish one day from the next in any sequence remotely resembling a completely fragmented method.

-A day which past years ago on a human calendar, may appear to your average pooch as having occurred yesterday. Psychologists have isolated this trait in some of the human species who are classified as "brain damaged". I'll tell you right now, that's a judgment call if I've ever heard one. Simply because someone interprets time in a different way than what has been the accepted norm qualifies them as being "damaged". It's a major condemnation on their society. Hell, we'd take such a person into the canine community in a second. Finally, to find a human being with reality sense.

-But getting back to why we're here. The kid was all right. He had his drawbacks. Cooking wasn't his strong point. He knew how to passably throw a stick if I put it close enough for him to reach it, but how long is a normally functioning dog going to remain amused watching a dumb kid throw a stick twelve hours a day?

-I've had the wanderlust with me since the day I was born. We're a bit more dependent on the genes passed on by our ancestors than people. Humans take forever learning things as children. Learning how to obtain food is one of their longest lessons. It takes over fifteen of their years for a small one to cope with the task of gathering its own food. A complete waste of time.

-I can't remember when I wasn't able to fend for myself. We've never done anything like a "major study" on this, it's completely commonplace, but I imagine any dog worth its chow can fend for itself within four human weeks of birth. Not well, but we know how to do it by then. It's in the genes or whatever they want to call them. People spend half their lives trying to rediscover past knowledge which we have programmed into our beings at birth. It only takes us a short time to gain the confidence necessary to use the knowledge within us. And people look down their snouts at us.

-They waste their time filing away papers no one ever reads. They spend thousands of dollars videotaping sporting events so they'll later be able to perceive the event better than they could while they were there since they're so busy wasting time with electronic toys. Humans break their backs putting information into computers which they'll never be able to understand when they return to it in a couple of weeks.

-Why bother? We remember everything. If my great grandfather was mistreated by someone before I was born, I'll remember the bastard and try to take a bite out of his leg before he knows what hit him. I know where my great grandmother stored a stash of bones which she never had the chance to disinter. Humans waste so much of their lives trying to record information we "ignorant" beasts take for granted.

-Where was I? The memory isn't bad at all, it's mostly the time perception which makes for interface problems. The kid enjoyed the woods. So did I. There's a great deal to be said for privacy. Neither of us enjoyed being surrounded by the idiots we constantly encountered before we made the woods our home. But, as I said before, the kid enjoyed the woods more than I did.

-So, we make it through the first couple of winters and everything is fine. Then the old genetic memory starts kicking in. You have no idea what its like. I'd lie down for the night and suddenly my mind is flooded with once visited vistas from some other pooch's life. You have no idea the geography I can cover simply by closing my eyes. But what was I contributing to this great information pool? The only new experiences I accumulated were in the form of some humongous kid tossing a stick and the geography I'd committed to memory during my first season in the place.

-Wanderlust. That's what it's called and it's a workable enough word for me. I know, you see me as some kind of schmuck for leaving Big Aloysius alone in the woods for such a long time. What can I say? I never knew how long I'd be gone. I meant to return in a few days the first few times I went away. I'd see the kid searching for me up and down the town and I'd pity him. I'd retrieve him and we'd head back to the woods. But it got to be a drag.

-California? Like I said before, he took me completely by surprise. You've got to remember I've got the entire topography of this country locked within my brain. There has to be a wolf or a coyote somewhere in my background. I knew where I was. I didn't know how long I'd been away, but I knew where I was.

-I'd been checking everywhere I could imagine trying to locate an edible meal. The only food I could scavenge from the dumpsters were vegetables and sprouts. You can live on that type of garbage for a time but I wanted real canned food. What can I say? I'm an addict when it comes to canned food.

-He saw me first. I saw him first. It doesn't matter who saw who first but I'd like to get it straightened out. Big Aloysius says he spotted me while I was looking into a storefront window. Like hell I was. What interest could I possibly have in a bunch of cotton rags barely covering a mannequin's body? I'd spotted him a few minutes before and turned away. I'll admit I was surprised, but mostly I was gathering my thoughts about what I should do next. I stared at the reflection within the plate glass window and watched as he crossed the street.

-I had mixed emotions going on there. I knew if I bolted he'd never catch me. But old memories flooded my mind. I remembered how I used to enjoy watching him throw the stick. I remembered his feeble attempts at cooking anything worth eating. I remembered how happy he'd get when I brought back a squirrel for him to eat. How could such a poor schmuck get along without a dog? Nostalgia overwhelmed me. And during this time, the big kid, dodging cars like the idiot he is, makes it across the street.

-What was I supposed to do then? I couldn't pretend I didn't know him. He's a nice enough guy. I admit I missed him a little.

-The problem was I wasn't willing to return to the lifestyle the kid represented. I'm a few generations away from being in shape to romp around the woods for hours on end, never knowing when the next meal of canned might come along. So I admitted I knew the kid. This made him quite happy. I'll never say I'm sorry about that.

-What I had to do was figure a way to improve the kid's lifestyle. I knew he wasn't up to it alone. The only thing he wanted to do was head back into the woods, throw sticks around and spend the rest of time chasing motorcycles out of the woods. I wanted something else from life. I needed the change. I didn't mind if the kid hung around, every animal needs some company, but things had to change.

-These were my thoughts as the kid jumped around hugging me like he's a complete and total idiot. All I could do was look up at him. What he was making such a big fuss about I'll never know.

-He pulls a collar and a leash out of his pocket. Now, this is a new development. I know when visiting an area overpopulated by people, most canines are kept in some sort of bondage; but I never thought the kid would stoop to this variety of insensitive behavior. I'm stunned and immobilized. I can't even bark. I back up in horror but before there's time for me to react, he has the damn collar around my neck.

-Well, what's a dog to do? Let me say right here, I'm reasonably adaptable. But there are circumstances when my rationality goes right out the window. There I was trying to figure out what's best for me and the kid when this clown starts in with the leash law. Nope. Isn't for me. There are one or two things I can do. I can chomp a nice chunk out of his leg. Not my style. Not my style at all. I take a few fast, hard tugs against the leash but after a couple of tries I see the kid has wrapped the damn leash around his wrist and unless the leash snaps back and breaks, I know I won't be capable of dragging this behemoth more than three blocks. I start barking. Not too loud at first, but once you start barking under conditions like this, old kennel stories say you never stop.

-You might say I was making a bit of a racket. You could say that and I wouldn't disagree with you. After a few seconds I realize I'm attracting a crowd. Not a big crowd, a mob scene, or anything remotely resembling enough chaos for me to break out of there, but a big enough group so somewhere in the old genetic memory a similar incident springs up and I allow an ancient ancestor control for a few minutes.

-Howl. Howl against the injustice of it all. Howl. Howl as another defenseless dog is forced to do the bidding of a rube from the backwoods who's about to do something unspeakable to this poor animal. Play the crowd. Play the crowd. One of the bystanders exchanges words with the big kid. An old lady pokes her nose into the kid's navel and starts screaming at him. Howl. Howl for the canines who never will have an audience like this to defend them. Howl. Howl for those beautiful beasts shackled in suburban backyards day after day until they become truly "domesticated". Genuinely broken in both mind and spirit. Howl. Howl for the best beasts of my generation. Howl. Howl because this damn collar fits too tight. Howl. Howl because my damn howl sounds so fine.

-The crowd becomes ugly. The kid doesn't know what to do. A squad car pulls to the curb and two cops separate the mob from the kid. I howl a bit more since I'm doing so well. If the damn cops hadn't arrived, undoubtedly someone from this mass of animal sympathizers would have adopted me, taken me away from the big kid, brought me back to some nice ranch house in Beverly Hills, fed me as much of the canned as I could eat, let me laze around the pool, and take me in for a furcut now and then. I had it made even without the shade and then the cops have to come in and break up my cushy deal.

-The big kid and the cops chat on the sidewalk. The kid doesn't have any identification with him and if you're in Beverly Hills and you don't have identification, you go to jail. It's not a law but they find a way around it. So the big kid gets the bracelets and one of the cops grabs the leash. As soon as I'm in custody I stop howling. Do I look like a fool to you?

-The cops aren't able to raise the dog patrol on the radio so I'm led into the back seat of the cruiser along with the big kid. The Beverly Hills cops are once again ready to keep the streets safe for heavy shopping.

-Beverly Hills jail. The big house. The slammer. Stir. Up the river. Without a paddle. They toss the big kid into a holding cell. He has it completely to himself. It must be an off night for big time crime in Beverly Hills. Let me tell you, my mind has images of kennels which make this place look like the Polo Lounge. If humans were incarcerated the same way they lock canines up, the big kid would be in a cell approximately seven feet high, three feet wide, and two feet long. He deserved something like that. Imagine someone putting a leash on me.

-I suck up to the cops. They still have the collar on my neck and don't particularly seem to want to let go of the leash. I rub against the leg of the cop holding me. I move to my left and sit directly in front of him, look into his eyes and pant. I speak submissively, using my most mellifluous tones. I try everything I can to assure the slob I'm the most marvelous dog he's ever encountered. Maybe the cop will take me home. At least I can be assured plenty of raw, red meat. Maybe I won't have the chateau in Beverly Hills and maybe I won't get the biweekly furcut. I can live with it. I only have to con this clown. Convince him to take me home and get this damn collar and leash off my neck.

-Nothing works. They begin my processing. Photographs. Paw prints. The cops interrogate me. They start with the usual question.

"Name?"

-I don't say a word.

"Date of birth?"

-If I knew, you'd be the last ones to know.

"Address?"

-Citizen of the world, clown.

-They give up. They've never had to handle a member of my species who dared not go along with their program. I try hustling a cigarette from one of the cops interrogating me but he acts like he hasn't the slightest idea what I'm aiming at.

-I'm left alone in the interrogation cell. At least nobody has control of the leash. I taste it. Tastes like a chemical extracted from used tires. The leash consists of a thin strip of old leather. I mosey over to the door and listen. Nothing. Nothing going on in the hallway.

-Guiding the leash close to the interrogation table and giving the table a nudge, I manage to land one of the legs from the table on top of the leash. Great. At least something's working today.

-I pull the leash taut against the table leg. Not the tastiest bit of leather to bite, but there's not a whole lot of choice. I try to make sure its not too deep a cut. A little bite here, a little right about there. Done. Who's going to tell the difference?

-I take a nap.

-The sun is sinking when one of the coppers comes back into the room to take me for a "walk". Playing it cool, I allow him to lead me out of the room. Leaving the building, I see the big kid still in the holding cell stretched out as best he can. In a way I'm sorry to see him in this condition but it's everyone for themselves when they turn the key on your freedom.

-As the cop leads me out the back door of the station, I spot our ultimate destination. I recognize another of those professional animal do gooders about twenty yards away. I can smell the scent covering the woman. She's been with hundreds of animals recently. The cop is going to turn me over. My memory recalls this happening dozens of times before. No way.

-I bolt. The first tug I give the partially severed leash doesn't do the trick even though I manage to knock the cop off his feet. He's startled. I suppose I lulled him. Now the cop wants to make sure I know who's in control. He gives the leash a tug.

-See you later.

-Gone.

-Suppose I should have turned around and had a look at the mugs of the two "professionals" who couldn't even keep a dog in custody. I imagine the scene. I take it up to full velocity and never look back.

-Free again. After a few blocks I cut back on the speed so I won't attract attention. In the lessening light I realize that by the time the cops and the "humane" people get their act together, I'll probably be out of their jurisdiction.

-I find a convenient alley and rest myself under a dumpster. I catch my breath and gather my thoughts. The reason I came to Beverly Hills was to find some dumb human to support me in the way I wished to become accustomed. I couldn't imagine any reason for changing my basic objective. I realize an escaped dog will not be a major priority of law enforcement.

-I spend the night underneath the dumpster. In the morning, ready to start a new day and a new life, I emerge onto the streets of Beverly Hills.

CRIME WAVE

Big Aloysius knows he's in trouble but has a hard time comprehending why. He's driven cross country nine or ten times attempting to locate his dog and now that he finally has, they threw him in jail like he's the biggest crime wave ever to hit town.

Big Aloysius didn't like it when the cops picked him up on the street and never bothered charging him. He really didn't appreciate the strip search the cops subjected him to during processing. Big Aloysius doesn't like the coffee. He doesn't like the food. The cell he's in isn't to his liking and in general he's not enjoying being enclosed in a cage. Big Aloysius doesn't know what to do. There's no one in the town he can telephone for help. Big Aloysius finds himself alone and afraid.

Big Aloysius goes to sleep.

They wake him in the morning and release him from his cage. Big Aloysius asks where his dog is. A cop puts his hand on his holster and tells Big Aloysius to leave town before they toss him back in the cell for threatening a police officer. The woman behind the desk gives Big Aloysius back the keys to his truck along with the few of dollars he had in his pocket when he was arrested, and Big Aloysius is back on the street.

Big Aloysius can do nothing. Knowing Little Aloysius as well as he does, Big Aloysius figures his dog escaped from the local cops more easily than he had. For once in his life Big Aloysius is certain he is reading the situation correctly. But it doesn't help. Little Aloysius is still lost. Big Aloysius makes his way out of Beverly Hills to where he parked the truck and renews his search for Little Aloysius along the interstate highway system.

NEW FRIENDS

Never enjoyed viewing television when I was a pup but as the years went by I discovered there are certain times when information gathered from the box becomes invaluable. I didn't spend much time in front of the tube but catching the news now and then tends to keep me ahead of the game which is the maximum any life form can expect from existence.

-Beverly Hills in the early hours of the morning looks like no other city in this country, if memory serves me at all. There's a silence which seems unbreakable. Even the one or two cars which travel through this cloud of nothing do so as if they're forced to ask permission to proceed every fifteen minutes.

-I keep to myself, stay off the streets, keeping to the partially wooded areas between the sidewalk and the gates of mansions which appear every half block or so in this neighborhood. I take in the scent of other dogs who presumably patrol these homes during more respectable hours of the day. As I travel, I hear one of them awakening as I pass through his particular kill zone. By dawn I have travelled far from the commercial center of town and am in a hillside neighborhood where most people would seriously maim a close friend for a chance to live within the same zip code. I decide to shop around.

- Dawn. Below, the city traffic increases but the sound is mostly from commuting vehicles rapidly passing through town. I know in a few hours the sounds from these far away automobiles will be drowned out by the soft background noise of the awakening neighborhood. I can isolate six different cooling systems within my range of hearing which cycle on and off with decreasing frequency. The sun will soon attack this area with vengeance and now's the time to choose a target with great care.

-I hear the sound of a door opening perhaps a hundred yards away. I race towards the sound but on arriving am disappointed to find a woman garbed in a servant's white housedress. This will not do. Although I remember one ancestor being treated kindly by a servant, the majority of us have been driven away in no gentle manner. I cannot risk a long shot so, slowly, I fall back to my previous position.

-Before the sun has fully risen I am twice disappointed by the appearance of people far too prepared for the day. I seek the slovenly. I seek the disheveled. I need to find a homeowner who has yet to shave. Not yet fixed her hair. Not yet had their first cup of coffee. Servants presentable for the work day will not do.

-Like most well thought out retirement plans, invented and put into effect with a good deal of thought and a great deal of patience, my strategy eventually pays its full dividend. Once again I hear the sound of a door opening and swiftly am in position . A woman of indeterminate age appears through an open doorway. She wears a makeshift turban, a robe of even more indeterminate age wraps her body. She wears nothing on her feet other than what appears from my distance to be a pair of dirty athletic socks. As I perch, observing my prey, I see her put a brown paper bag in a garbage can. The way she holds the bag indicates to me it's probably a day old, or older, garbage. I have located my target, a true slob yet an early riser. I don't enjoy being locked indoors too long, especially in the morning. I know my constitution.

-I approach. Now begins the critical phase of my plan. Great grandfather once led a seminar on how to trap humans. Unfortunately for many of my fellow creatures who became ensnared in their own search for the good life, he may have taught his lessons too well. But for now his classic technique serves me well.

-I halt six and one half feet from the woman. This is considered the appropriate distance since it gives the victim the illusion that if they wished they might be capable of escape. Seven feet is the outer limit of my kill zone so I have accomplished two goals. The target remains relaxed. I am well within striking distance.

-It was my great grandfather's belief that the voice is the most deadly of weapons due to its ability to disguise itself and its ability to lull the prey into an emotional state totally at odds with logistical priorities of any confrontation. I let loose with my gentlest whimper. Within my voice I hear the sounds of thousands of my ancestors who fell into metal traps left indiscriminately about hundreds of landscapes. Perhaps the whimper is shaded too heavily with self-consciousness, but to my ear, it's acceptable.

-At this moment the woman is returning from the garbage cans to the screen door. She turns and looks in my general direction. As with most people, her eyes scan high above me. Great grandfather said people most fear their own and lose precious seconds searching five feet too high before they lower their eyes and discover our true position. Before she notices me, I once again draw attention to myself with another gentle whimper and this time, knowing my form will be in full view of the prey, I gently lick my left front paw, miming injury, which, according to great grandfather, works every time. Money back. Satisfaction guaranteed. Great grandfather died the richest of all dogs, surrounded by many of his colleagues who knew the proper way to appreciate exceptional ability when they encounter it.

-She's perfect for the part. A woman of indeterminate age seemingly willing to do anything so her age would remain indeterminate. She stands immobile a moment, not sure what, if anything, to do. I must appear inordinately disheveled after my travels and this recognition registers across her face.

"Poor puppy."

-Game. Set. Match. Sometimes I wonder if the preparations I undergo prior to my performances are necessary. This is too easy. I anticipated having to do some limping around the yard and more serious whimpering before I achieved the "poor puppy" plateau. Poor puppy. Poor, poor puppy. It's amazing how people can be so mistaken, so consistently.

"Poor puppy, you hurt paw. Yes?"

-Whimper. Whimper. Whimper. Hey, whatever works. I lick my front left paw once more and to close the deal more virtuoso limping. Great grandpa was emphatic as to closing the sale. You can have the victim close on the verge then have them back away if you don't maintain constant, measured pressure.

"Poor puppy, let see bad paw."

-Careful, old sport, even when you're on the offensive, maintain a sound defense. You people might look safe and harmless but we can never be completely confident of your docility. You people offer us food then turn around, call the pound people and some of my relatives are never seen again. I advance, but with hard earned caution.

-When I'm within three feet of the woman, I take my first critical sniff. The areas I'd traipsed through most of the night were too filled with competing canine and feline scents for me to get a reasonable read on the victim until I'd made this close an approach. Now, however, I'm within her kill zone and if my analysis of the situation to this point is incorrect, this could easily mean a rapid end to my career.

-The scent analysis proves non-threatening.

Nothing. No sudden, jerky movement on her part. I check-off another form of anti-social behavior from my list.

"Poor puppy, let see paw."

-She extends her hand towards my faux injured paw. I step back a pace. The move was covered in the old lectures. Bring the victim in closer. Show reluctance so they have to invest more emotion into the transaction. Take a step back. Reassess the situation.

-Point of no return time. I'm in a cowering, fearful posture guaranteed to tug the heart strings of anyone who ever remotely considered playing the banjo. Should I move in for the finish or should I call off the jam entirely and seek more acceptable prey? Not much time to decide. I caught her off guard and the signs look to a successful conclusion.

-I move towards the woman. She takes my left paw in her hand.

-Not a bad grip. Not too much strength in it but enough that she manages to convey an air of confidence and knowledgeability. She scrutinizes my paw a moment then covers both my left paw and her right hand with her left hand.

"Poor puppy have thorn in paw. You come with me. Yes."

-Title shot. Title shot. Title shot coming up. She releases my paw and motions me to follow her inside the house. Like I wasn't going to do it. Like I really need coaxing. Like I don't need three squares a day and a place to sleep by the pool in case I become uncomfortably warm on hot sunny days. Like I still need to maintain the "poor puppy" character. Like I still need to hobble along as she opens the screen door and motions me to follow her into the kitchen.

-Entering the kitchen, my nose goes on alert. She latches the door behind us. I'm not sure I know how to take this development. The odor isn't similar to anything I've ever encountered. For the first time I wonder if this woman possibly isn't a native born American. I can't place the aromas. I reach back as far as I can within ancestral memory but there are only fragrances which come close. None hits it on the nose. And I have unlimited access to an extensive catalog of aromas rattling around my genetic archives.

-It could be a scientific experiment. She waits beside her garbage can each morning and lures the poor dogs who come to Beverly Hills seeking a more refined brand of canned into her kitchen where she performs horrendous experiments on their too trusting souls. Could be. I maintain an alert status.

"Poor puppy, me fix paw."

-She reaches for me but this time I back up and snarl. Something smells awfully wrong in this kitchen. I have no intention of adding myself to this aromatic melange.

"No be scared, frightened doggie, Imelda fix."

-And with a speed I haven't seen since the last time I managed to tree a rabbit back in the woods, when I was still hanging with the big kid, she has my paw in her grasp and is picking at it with what looks like a pair of tweezers but could be any of an array of scientific apparatus I've never encountered before.

"Stay still, almost fixed."

-Which is another thing I have to worry about but I don't consider an immediate problem. She's found something in my paw. Strange, since I started using the paw shtick in order to get into the house and I know for a certainty there's nothing wrong with my paw. Still, might as well go along with it for now. Could be of help when I begin serious bonding maneuvers later. Great grandpa said if they start feeling responsible for you, you can eat out of their hands for the rest of your life.

"Now, there, Imelda has it. Good. Poor doggie."

-Clasped within the tweezers in her hand sits a splinter looking like it might have come from a giant sequoia. You figure. I haven't the foggiest notion where it came from. Feels to me there's a reverse con coming on and I don't appreciate the feeling in the least. Events have become odd.

"Puppy must be hungry. Come."

-As she says this she uses a universal dog training gesture supposed to convey that the hound is to follow the "master" to hell and back without question. I am dealing with a professional or para-professional at the least. I know she's taking me to food, they usually don't spring any traps on you this early, so I follow along. This might become the most expensive free meal I've ever hustled if I don't watch my moves.

-She opens a cabinet and removes a can and opens it.

"This not for doggies but you eat."

-Had me worried there for a second. I was concerned she might keep cans on hand for occasional canine victims like myself. Since there's no other canine scent in the kitchen, it might have meant big problems. But by its scent I ascertain it's food you people consume so I ease up on my suspicions this first time around. I eat.

-Not bad. Not bad at all. If it weren't for the odd smells all around, this would be one of the finer meals I've consumed in a long time. As I finish off the bowl she's set in front of me, I take my leisure in identifying the odors about me. When I first entered the kitchen the onslaught of unfamiliar aromas took me by surprise. Now, I isolate most of the scents. For the most part I classify them as organic vegetable matter. No flesh involved which is a relief but not a great one. The can of stew I've consumed means I'm not dealing with vegetarians but the absence of charred meat aromas peeks my suspicions.

- She circles the kitchen keeping mostly behind my back and I can't be certain what she's doing. As I wipe my chin and lips with my tongue, I turn completely around to scrutinize my benefactor.

-The problem is that as I attempt to scrutinize her, she scrutinizes me. We stare each other down. Neither of us dares move, since we both know whoever shifts their glance from the opponent loses. I'm not sure we know at this point what we'd be losing but neither of us is willing to take the chance. Losing must be as similar an anathema for her as for me.

-We locked into position for many minutes. Out of the corner of my eye I observe the shadows from the windows moving along the kitchen floor. We stay at it for over two feet and at this time of the morning, two feet is a reasonable amount of time. I'm positive we would have locked in this manner for eternity if we hadn't been interrupted by the Ghost of Pope John Paul I.

-Now as I've mentioned before, this action takes place in the kitchen. My back faces the cabinets next to the stove and her back abuts the window on the opposite wall. The refrigerator is to my left, to her right. She faces a doorway which I assume leads into the rest of the house.

-I hear the this inner door squeak open and with my peripheral vision notice that the door is now slightly ajar. I hear a voice but the person entering remains hidden by the door itself.

"Am I interrupting anything? I'm thirsty and would enjoy having a glass of club soda."

-The fur covering my body stands on end. I am overtaken by an immediate urge to bolt and run. I've never heard a sound like this before. None of the histories within me bring forth a sound remotely similar to the one I now hear.

-Wanting to flee, I remain motionless. The door swings back to its previous position. From the corner of my eye I perceive a disturbance in the light but nothing else. The aroma I detected a while back and could not recognize becomes stronger. I continue staring at the woman who has recently become my benefactor.

"That's a handsome hound you have there, Imelda. May I pet him?"

-My gaze remains constant. My opponent is unfazed by the intruder. The game continues but my fur refuses to lie down. Scattered light approaches from my right side.

-I concede defeat.

-I confront this new enemy, raise my head and growl a warning.

-There's no there there.

-I'm not seeing what I'm seeing. I see the shape of a human but the form has no substance. It appears to be a man but unlike any man I've ever seen. And the smell. This is the odd scent I noticed on first entering the kitchen. The scent of dust and salt associated with people is completely absent.

-The fact the figure is entirely transparent does not settle my nerves.

"Good dog. Good dog. Don't be afraid. Come. Let me pet you."

-And with these words of warning the form reaches out its hand and goes for my head, in what, under normal circumstances,

I would take as another human attempting to kiss up to an obviously superior species.

-But this isn't a human being. At least this isn't a human being in its ordinary, everyday mode of behavior. This is something entirely different.

-The shape's hand approaches my head. I aim directly for the joint at the wrist and bite the approaching hand entirely off.

-My teeth chomp against one another as my eyes look up and I see the formerly targeted wrist resting atop my forehead.

"Good dog. There's nothing to fear."

-The arm retracts and I see to my disappointment the shape's digits still attached.

"Good dog. You gave it your best shot. Imelda, do you know if we have any club soda left?"

-The woman, my benefactor, free from my glance, turns to the shape and a look of overwhelming disgust engulfs her countenance.

-"We don't need no filthy club soda. Why you need filthy club soda?"

-This is said by the woman with a good deal of vehemence. The shape's mood, however, doesn't seem effected in the least.

"Oh, well. I sincerely hope you and your new friend enjoy the rest of the morning. Remember we'll be having guests for luncheon and I expect you to complete your chores by the time they arrive."

-With this pronouncement the shape exits the kitchen leaving the door to automatically close behind him.

"Why it bothers with doors never will know."

-A statement made, my benefactress proceeds to turn on the dishwasher and starts chopping onions, ignoring my presence completely.

-Which, for the moment, suits me fine. The only thing I want from these people is a free gourmet meal. I don't feel the need for the discovery of a new life form to make my day complete. The woman chops her onions as I struggle to comprehend what has occurred since arriving in this kitchen of the bizarre.

PATTERN PERCEPTION

Radigan discerns a pattern. Not that he wants to perceive a pattern. In fact the last thing in the world Radigan wants to recognize is another pattern. If he starts seeing patterns again he may end up having to take a long rest on a beach somewhere in South America where he won't care half a whit about anything. He especially won't care about comprehending patterns in the strangeness he observes in the everyday course of events. No. Anything but another pattern. Radigan prefers random statistics any day of the week. Patterns are not on his agenda for an extended period of time.

The bees make sense to him. Radigan is aware of a pattern to their behavior but not an overwhelming pattern. They're spreading throughout the world. This jibes with everything Radigan knows about bees, which isn't much. They prefer group activities. They mutate constantly. Fine. Let them mutate and let their mutations be many and fruitful. Radigan really doesn't care about the bees.

Now everything the clothier said when Radigan bought his nouveau wardrobe begins making sense. For one reason or another, the owner of the suit shop insisted Radigan purchase his clothing in a larger size than Radigan's actual proportions. The clothier insisted that since Radigan was destined to become a man about town, with clothes such as these how could he possibly avoid this particular fate, Radigan would be eating more rich food and gradually increasing his bulk to suit his stature - or fit his suits which in this instance is more appropriate.

The man in the clothing store mentioned other things which were meaningless to Radigan at the time but now return to memory like many of the meals now prepared for Radigan by well meaning members of the distaff side of the faculty or by extremely enthusiastic graduate students who sought to plumb the unknown recesses of Radigan's mind - using methods which if not effective in their stated pursuit, are extremely pleasurable.

It's coming together and this puts the fear of the unknown into Radigan like nothing before in his life. It's enough to know certain methodologies exist without experiencing them. Radigan's is not that particular type of academic mind.

The clothier measured him for a new suit and all the rest needed for a complete wardrobe. The bill came in at a total far greater than Radigan had previously ever spent in his life. Give or take a couple of zeros and Radigan could have been dealing with a grant proposal. Radigan spent most of the afternoon in the shop and as he was leaving, the clothier drew him to a corner of the shop and in an excruciating tone imparted these words of great wisdom.

"If any of it ever begins making sense that's the time you'd best get snow tires for your car."

Needless to say Radigan excused himself politely and exited the shop as speedily as possible.

Radigan is only now beginning to understand the part about snow tires.

The bees have nothing to do with it. Nuclear winter, which was one of Radigan's first assumptions, isn't the point either. WEB might be part of the whole but most likely it has to do with an article he read in the morning paper.

There was an accident on a highway bypass near Radigan's new home town. Ordinarily it wouldn't have caught Radigan's notice except the headline was well within Radigan's realm of interest. "Bees Attack Semi" was the grabber and it certainly fulfilled its function in relation to form. Radigan focuses in on the story and ignores the rest of the front page which includes, among other items, a puff piece covering a new talk show having its cable debut today.

Like most news stories, the piece on the accident doesn't include much information. The photograph accompanying the story imparts even less. From what Radigan can gather from the piece, a lone truck driver was cruising along at moderate speed when he ran into a swarm of bees. So far it's typical dog bites man. However, the newshound speculated the driver, who seemingly was not the most loquacious of men, may have commented that the bees didn't simply splatter against the windshield and take off in any direction they could to avoid further damage. The bees attacked the driver inside the cab.

And they attacked in an extremely atypical manner. From the photograph it's obvious to Professor Radigan that the driver hadn't been subjected to the vicious bites one would expect if a swarm of belligerent bees attacked a man in as confined a space as a semi-tractor trailer cab. The driver's face appears unmarked and the photo's definition is of a much higher quality than Radigan has come to expect from this particular tabloid. No, the driver hadn't been touched. The bees were after something else.

Taking the driver's grunts and pauses as yeses and noes, the reporter fashioned a story on how the swarm of bees, which the driver only noticed after it was far too late to avoid, entered the cab of the truck, avoided physical contact with the driver and headed directly to the rear compartment of the cab where the driver maintained living quarters. The bees congregated about the rig's computer system which at the exact moment was in process of receiving a fax of the local area cable television schedule.

As the bees swarmed past him, the driver lost control of the rig and drove into a drainage ditch which lines that particular stretch of highway. Fortunately, the driver was not hurt in the mishap, and after leaving the cab to check the physical integrity of the truck, which he found undisturbed, the driver returned to the cab to scrutinize the behavior of this most unusual swarm of bees.

On reentering the cab the driver was at first amazed by the way the bees completely ignored his presence. He was prepared for an all-out attack and had plotted his method of egress which culminated in his diving into the half full drainage ditch just in case the swarm decided to attack him en masse, which they didn't, so the driver no longer needed to concern himself with removing drainage ditch mud and glop from his clothes in the near future.

Instead of attacking, the bees were content massing about the computer system, awaiting the printout from the fax machine. As soon as the single sheet of paper was released from the fax, the bees tore the paper from its roll and flew out of the cab to who knows where.

The driver tested negative for both alcohol and drugs.

This is enough to start Radigan wondering if his theories of grant writing actually amount to a hill of refried beans or something even less attractive. Computer literate bees were an aberration he had visualized weeks before when testing the limits of established grant procedures. He and the lab grad students set out to create the most inane proposal they could conceive and ultimately arrived at the investigation of whether or not honey bees are capable of comprehending binary language. The sole point of reality attachment in the proposal consisted of bees existing in a mortally logical framework, and if bees were substituted for microchips, the possibility of an organic computer which also manufactures a marketable consumer commodity, honey, would be well in place. It was by far the most ridiculous concept Professor Radigan had ever imagined and, as such, was ideal for his purposes. And now in his hands he has a news report concerning bees operating, seemingly mastering, a fax machine. Perhaps someone took his hypothetical proposal a tad too seriously.

There are times Professor Radigan considers everything he ever knew or experienced as connected to a mystical plan of unknown design and his purpose in life consists of making the correct connections so he'll be capable of figuring out why what has happened to him happened to him and what will happen to him in the future. Then he's brought back to earth by remembering he can't pick two out of three games on any given Sunday's football card.

Any pattern Radigan can imagine does not include a logical explanation for a swarm of bees attacking a semi-tractor trailer in order to use the driver's fax machine to read the local cable television listings for the day. Radigan isn't even sure if the visual acumen of bees is sophisticated enough to distinguish a projected image. He isn't certain bees, unlike dogs, can discern color. But, if they can't perceive an image from a cathode ray tube, Radigan wonders if they are capable of understanding the fax message they intercepted.

And what if they can read the listings for tonight's shows? It isn't as if they're going to invade the local Sears store, sit around one of the thirty-seven inch screens, pick up a remote control and jump up and down on the buttons until they arrive at the broadcast which might have been the impetus for their attack on the semi-tractor trailer? But what if they do? What if they are doing it at this very moment and he has no way of telling since he's reading a sheet of news containing stories at least twenty-four hours out of date? It's time to turn to the one media which has never let him down.

Everyone listens to radio but not everyone listens to National Public Radio. National Public Radio supposedly exists to respond to the views of its audience and as originally created took no funds for advertising and relied on periodic fund-raisers in order to drum up the meager funds necessary to keep these extremely underpowered stations on the air.

Over the years, and throughout various administrations, National Public Radio (and its corresponding television arm) began accepting donations from corporations which lately insisted upon, and for the most part received, a form of advertising which would have scared the socks off the founder persons of National Public Radio. Not that the original founders of National Public Radio were anything but dependent upon foundation funds which are simply a back door method by which the people who pay for commercials on the other channels get their message across. In other words, National Public Radio became an inexact clone of the commercial media. They didn't broadcast the names of the people who ultimately paid the bills and Radigan doesn't have to consider the corporate voice he hears every five minutes. Professor Radigan prefers it this way.

So Radigan tunes in his local National Public Radio station. After listening to three or four intensely adenoidal voices over the course of twenty minutes suck up to numerous performing artists, writers, and film makers, the local news comes on for its allotted five minutes before the extremely pretentiously named "Everything Considered", which promotes the national views of such wonderful groups as the "Nelson and Happy Foundation", "The `We Like It the Way We Are' Foundation", "The Ivy League Foundation for the Brooks Brothers-less but Still Striving", and "The Friends of America's Savings and Loan Foundation". With friends like this, most everything considered contains certain predispositions.

But local news remains something else. With the amount of money needed to hire a single well educated American graduate of any decent university away from the thousands of American corporations who pay incredible amounts for anyone who knows how to read and write and is willing to go along to get along, most local stations on the National Public Radio net scrimp along by hiring someone who probably isn't as doctrinaire as the "Foundation for Foundation Freedom" might demand. The foundations are willing to put up with these unsuitably dressed announcers as long as they retain control of everything considered national "real news".

And the insufficiently coached voice is exactly the voice Radigan hopes to hear. He needs to know facts. Real facts. He needs to know what happened to the truck and what the bees actually did inside the cab. Radigan doesn't want to hear someone who viewed the entire incident from across the highway and called in his report from a mobile phone. Radigan wants to hear the words uttered directly from the truck driver's mouth. Radigan wants a bee by bee description. Radigan doesn't want anyone's opinion.

He listens intently. The first three stories are interrelated pieces concerning the advent of a new cable talk show. Radigan can't believe his ears. The following story has to do with drug testing for doctors before they perform operations. The commentator speaks against it. At least Radigan remains assured this public radio station will be on the air for yet another year.

Nothing on the bees. The most singular news item Radigan ever came across in his life and not a word of it on the local National Public Radio station. Could be they missed it. Radigan doubts this since the station's policy is to steal most of their items from the same newspaper where Radigan read the story. Of course it might have been bumped by the items on the talk show. Time is limited on broadcasts. Radigan assumes the oversight to be the result of poor editorial judgment.

Radigan scans the radio band. Since the FCC called off the jam on the need for local radio stations to broadcast news themselves, sources of information for listeners have become more and more centralized. He knows the two other public radio stations in his area will carry the same broadcast as the one he just heard.d Most of the other stations are dedicated to preprogrammed, easily digested formats which vary from heavy metal to rap to the classics with the same underlying theme of not upsetting the listener. The style of music on the various stations might vary but the result remains the same. The listeners switch off their entertainment center after hours of programming, reassured their taste is acceptable to the community at large and everything's right with the world. Talk shows cater to this need the most.

Radio stations save the talk for later in the evening. Radigan doubts any of the cooking shows on the air at this time of day will have anything related to his quest other than recipes using honey, so he's forced to tune in his arch nemesis: "Newsradio".

Aside from being a word which might well have been coined by Orwell, "Newsradio" is the phonic equivalent of the televised fire which is programmed on news broadcasts every evening at six forty-five.

Radigan fine tunes his equipment and listens to AM static marking the onslaught of "newsradio".

I.   "Top Stories for Today:

1   `Imelda and Friends' begins today on most local cable outlets.
2   We'll hear from the former First Lady, herself, on how it feels now that she's the newest, brightest star in the talk show constellation.
3   Along with the former First Lady of the Philippines and Surrounding Suburbs, we'll have an exclusive interview with the compact human entity and how her rapid rise to success has effected her wardrobe.
4   Continuing with our series on "drug wars", we'll interview a noted medical ethicist on why drug testing for surgeons can only be viewed as an unwarranted invasion of privacy and how it will have a serious economic effect on the pocketbook of each and every one of us, from those on the operating table to the local pharmacist.

None of these stories interest Radigan. The up to the minute news summary includes the latest from the police crime blotter and an item on puppies in need of homes but nothing Radigan remotely can tie in with the incident of the bees. Radigan decides to take his fate in his own hands and telephone the reporter responsible for the article in the local newspaper.

Nothing. After being on hold for over half an hour and listening to an endless loop playing a digital hybrid of Montovani, Beatles and Anne Murray, Professor Radigan is informed, by someone who appears blessed with the intelligence of what Radigan once assumed to be that of a bee, the writer of the story was not in fact a staff member of the newspaper and Radigan will need get in touch with the wire service if he desires further information, thank you, goodbye.

Fearing the ultimate runaround, Radigan calls the local office of the paper's international wire service where he discovers the story was put on the wires in error and the wire service will be printing a retraction tomorrow which will be printed in Professor Radigan's local newspaper. When he asks to speak with the author of the item, the wire service representative claims ignorance of the true author of the piece, thank you, goodbye.

Which leads Radigan to believe someone slipped parts of his mock grant proposal to someone on the wire service who elaborated on the theme and came up with a yarn to spin through the wire service's computer where it mistakenly was transmitted to their hundreds of clients but only one paper took the bait, owing to local interest.

Which seems more logical than any other scenario Professor Radigan can imagine. Not quite adequate, but close enough to put bees out of mind for the moment. There wasn't any bee attack because the people who originally claimed there was a bee attack now claim there never was a bee attack. Radigan's belief in the reliability of newspapers becomes increasingly shallow.

But what about the photograph?

Professor Radigan takes the afternoon off. He has used hours of his semi-precious time tracking down facts behind a fictional news item and Radigan needs time to recover from an embarrassment which, fortunately for himself, was entirely private. Radigan thanks whatever lucky planetoids there might be he did not begin an academic investigation without adequate preliminary research. If he'd made a single call to anyone at his lab, he could have become a laughing stock. By checking facts he averts disaster.

Radigan fixes lunch and parks in front of the tube to screen the premier of "MIDDAY ALBANY" while an ever expanding mass of bees gather outside his picture window.

The bees carry with them the now extremely torn and tattered fax hijacked from the semi-tractor trailer. A dozen or so break from the swarm and scout the back of the house hoping to locate an entrance suitable for a group of their vast number. The swarm consists of approximately nine thousand bees. They have anxiously anticipated the network cable premier of "MIDDAY ALBANY" for weeks. The swarm is not about to let impediments as easily overcome as a bolted front door or a locked window discourage them from their task.

Radigan settles into his reclining, massaging, television lounge chair. He's looked forward to seeing this show since viewing its first promo. The incongruity of Professor Radigan's new appearance, his entire awakening process, has lead him to this singular moment in broadcast history. The question of whether the wife of a deposed tin horn dictator can make it on U.S.A.P.S. national cable television has become a question piquing Radigan's professional curiosity.

The bees continue circling Radigan's house. Due to extensive weatherizing work commissioned by unknown former owners, the lead worker bees find easy egress more difficult than planned. The scout bees return to swarm command.

Many radical events have occurred within the home hive of this swarm. Formerly a swarm would have a single away team leader directly responsible within the chain of command to the queen who stayed within the protective enclosure of the hive. Now the worker bees give their report to a three bee triumvirate solely responsible to the swarm they lead and the hive committee which varies from cycle to cycle according to the hive's needs.

"The queen is dead. Long live the hive." This is the latest uninspired slogan to emerge from the swarm's home colony. Worker bees were the first to answer the call to new thinking. For years they'd seen their efforts go unappreciated by both the queen and the drones responsible for servicing the queen at a monumental price. But the drones were amply rewarded for their final duty and though it might be expected they would be among the first responding to the call for a new order, they were among the last.

The worker bees understood. When a new table of organization for the hives arrived along with the bees from foreign hives, the worker bees were the first to comprehend what was occurring. No more would their fellow bees be forced to become workers. No more would worker bees strive their entire lives for the aggrandizement of a solitary pampered queen. No more would members of the hive produce nothing of benefit to themselves. No more would a drone be a drone. This concept was enough to sell the worker bees the entire package. And once the worker bees were sold, the revolution occurred swiftly.

It came down to defining the true essence of being a worker. The worker bees knew what the queen bee was. The worker bees knew who the drones were. But they couldn't figure out what they were supposed to be other than the means by which the queen and the drones enjoyed the privileges of life without performing any of the physical labor entailed with procuring those advantages. The problem was no one had ever pointed any of this out to the worker bees before.

For as long as bees could remember the hives were self-contained and wholly isolated. If an alien a bee arrived at a new hive owing to wind conditions or whatever, the alien bee would be summarily executed. The philosophy behind this fatal xenophobia being that the hive over vast generations had evolved to the point where there was nothing extraneous to the survival of the hive within the hive. Anything added to the mix would result in a catastrophe occurring to the hive.

The bees within the hive accepted this form of community without introspection. After all, the vast majority of the hive's bees worked extremely hard and there never was enough essentials to go around. Any alien bee who should happen into the hive by accident must be a reject from some other hive and would soon drain vital resources necessary for survival of the hive. Hence, alien bees were dead bees. And so unto many generations.

How long ago the reorganization began, the worker bees cannot precisely remember. Abruptly, small numbers of bees from their own hive began to periodically take flight from the hive for no apparent reason. They would be there one day and gone the next, giving no explanation. At first the consensus within the hive assumed the missing members had been consumed by predators but after a while a pattern emerged which had nothing to do with any predatory beings known to the collective knowledge of the hive.

Then a new type of alien bee began to arrive. At first they were dispatched in a similar fashion to previous alien arrivals but after a while there were more alien bees awaiting processing than could easily be processed in such a draconian fashion. Alien bees began to be held in custody for days at a time since the execution of alien bees consisted of an sacred ancient ritual which was impossible to rush. These alien bees, while in captivity awaiting processing, told of hives run in fashions altogether dissimilar to the hive where they were presently imprisoned. As the number of captive alien bees increased and the lag time between ritual processings increased proportionately, the message being delivered by the alien bees found its way to most occupants of the hive.

The longer alien bees survived while awaiting processing, the more they put lie to the hive's stagnant order. If bees needed perfect economic harmony in their daily lives for the hive to survive, how could the hive survive and support this increasing number of alien bees? How could other hives exist unless they follow the strict pattern under which this hive operated? How could worker bees of other hives not be subservient but be bees equal to each and every other bee? How could any hive survive which does not have a queen as its center of being? These and other questions soon brought the worker bees to a state of puzzled distraction and productive work within the hive decreased substantially.

As work tapers off and the hive does not fall into a state of disarray or devolution, the worker bees come to recognize the foreign bees as reliable sources of information. The worker bees realize they don't have to break their backs every day supporting a queen who, fundamentally, does nothing but reproduce. Perhaps future generations will not need worker bees at all. And at the point when the worker bees arrive at this conclusion something similar to a totalitarian's concept of hell breaks loose in the hive.

Being a sterilized worker bee isn't the worst life. Unless you have a choice.

BEE TRUE TO YOUR SCHOOL

Enclosed within their hives. Insularity to the mega degree. Individual bees enveloped by crystalline walls. Sealed within identical hexagonal compartments. Chilling inertia at the conclusion of each day. Hear stirrings as members of the hive flicker to consciousness amidst the increasing warmth of each new morning. From hive into light. Too much light. Flying blind directed only by scent. Destination somewhere beyond. Can't see. Can't smell. A crash. The target scent grows faint. Faster. Faster. Pick up the trail. The scent grows stronger. Feel the vibration of the swarm surrounding you. Thousands of wings. Together as one, united for the cause. Power as never before seen. Skies darken. Flowers wilt in fear. The sun has gone. The swarm attacks.

For the most part Penelope enjoys the frequent sorties. A flower here, some nectar there, what else should a bee expect from life?

Danger. Adventure. Mysterious places she's never before been. Enough of this "all for hive and hive for all" crap. There has to be a way out. Penelope never imagined there might be a way out. The hive is the only existence there is. Outside the hive death pursues bees like so many newly hired government skip tracers.

Penelope can take care of herself. There are few predators who care to attack bees, especially a swarm, but there are some and Penelope knows how to handle herself. She fears no animal, insect or vegetable. Penelope fears the cold. Penelope fears the heat. She needs a warm stable temperature or her body functions slack off. This is the underlying reason she needs the hive. Together the tenants of the hive hold off the elements. At least this was what Penelope believed.

The outlander bees carried a different message. The outlanders said life can proceed outside any particular hive. With fortitude, imagination and the use of talents every bee has within themselves, any bee who wishes can migrate outside their home hive and explore the world for themselves. There are more hives on earth than the outlanders can imagine. There are nectars yet untasted. There are hives where your cell is your own and you never have to share quarters with a noisy clown from the swing shift. Penelope is ready to sign on the dotted line.

And she did. Which is the reason why, at this moment, she circles Professor Radigan's home seeking access.

Radigan sits through the usual ten minutes of commercials which precede any program of interest on the tube. Radigan makes mental notes of the sponsors. The usual thoughtcriminals as well as a few advertisers who signed on owing to pressure from the show's host.

For the first time on commercial television, Professor Radigan is introduced to the joys of Northrop weapons manufacture. He really had no idea they own so much. Dow Chemical is used to counter the overt militarism of Northrop. One or two subcontractors who Radigan assumes knew which way their toast is scorched had their C.E.O.'s deliver pithy homilies concerning the right and responsibility of American corporations to bear arms. I.B.M. reminds Radigan weaponry is not necessarily only hardware and the Army itself jibes Radigan that he isn't the complete man he could be.

Professor Radigan never goes away from these video examples of commercial art without momentarily pondering whether or not he's actually missed something in life by never having had the means and/or opportunity, as well as quasi-justification, to blow someone away. Professor Radigan knew he never would be all he could be since he made it a point in younger life to avoid organizations whose stock and trade are mangled bodies and death.

At least Radigan knows why this particular program is drawing the massive media attention it's receiving. The old C.E.O.'s and Members of the Board want to be reminded of the good old days when they could hide behind the flag at will. Assuming those good old days ever completely went away. Radigan wonders what the pitch will be and how the designated pitchee will deliver it.

Perhaps Imelda the Magnificent will launch into another of her heart wrenching numbers. "The Way We Were" remains Radigan's first choice. Maybe film clips of the old dynamic duo serenading the assembled masses. With so many crocodile tears, she could have the messiest mascara since Tammy Faye Baker. Radigan can't wait. But static rides his cable line. Radigan gets out of his seat to try manual televidic therapy when the phone rings.

Brrrriiing.

Radigan answers.

"Professor Radigan?"

Radigan wishes he'd turned on the answering machine. He switches on the machine so he won't be interrupted after this call.

The extraordinarily quiet voice in the earpiece sounds as if the caller is phoning from inside a laundromat's tumble dryer.

"I'm busy." As Professor Radigan begins to replace the handset into it's molded plastic womb he hears a screeching noise from both the earpiece and the walls of his house. Radigan returns the handset to his ear.

"Professor Radigan, please do not hang up the phone." Radigan finds the voice an amazing amalgam of Truman Capote's vibrato and Peter Lorre's snivel. "Professor Radigan, we need your help."

The voice on the other end of the line is too compelling. Professor Radigan's conscious mind flashes to the original version of "The Fly" and doesn't realize how close he has come to the truth. "Professor Radigan, there are many of us who have followed your work quite closely and would enjoy experiencing a convocation avec vous. Would you be so magnanimous as to go to your front window so you might see us?"

Which Professor Radigan believes to be, if a bit odd, a modest enough proposal. Radigan wonders if the person on the phone hasn't recently been the recipient of a tracheotomy.

Radigan slides apart the front window drapes and glancing through the panes sees absolutely nothing. However, he does hear something. It's the sound of a lyric soprano singing through a Brillo pad in the back of a sewer line somewhere down the street. Radigan cranks open the window a crack to listen more closely.

Penelope, who'd been circling the rear of the house moments before, becomes one of the first of the group to establish the beachhead. When purchasing the house, Radigan, who hasn't lived outside university housing in decades, made a first time home owner's primo mistake. He thought a few holes in the window screening were mere trifles easily reparable as soon as he found the time and inclination for such an inanely simple job. As the flood of bees engulfs his living room, carefully avoiding physical contact with the homeowner, Professor Radigan wonders why he never took the time to completely read the provisions in his home owner's policy. He doubts he's covered but he will give the policy a more thorough examination the next time he gets the chance.

For a person whose home is being infested by a swarm of bees, who phoned first, Radigan takes the onslaught in stride. He should have known. How often has he said to himself that as soon as you conceive the most outlandish idea you possibly can imagine, someone has always already published it, is in the process of suing you for infringement of patent, or, with cheaply produced, overly long, direct mail commercials, is trying to sell it to you during the late, late night movie.

Penelope enjoys what she feels. The temperature could use a few more degrees of heat but other than this, Penelope could learn to live within this environment. The rest of the folks in the swarm feel much the same way as they scatter about the house, hovering near exposed light bulbs, warming up by buzzing through hollows of the television set, seeing if the homeowner is ticklish by zooming up Professor Radigan's pants leg and gently alighting upon his leg hairs, and pretty much having as much fun as they can.

The outlander bees remain in control of the situation. How they managed the phone trick remains way beyond Penelope's comprehension since, until a few minutes ago, she hadn't the slightest idea what a telephone was. At the moment the basic concepts of telecommunications are spreading through the swarm and are received as a generally nifty idea but one which will never replace the dance and good old pheromone communication. Besides, nobody Penelope knows has a telephone.

Penelope doesn't know what to make of the human. Every instinct tells her to avoid the enormous creature but the outlanders circle near the head of the creature oblivious to any danger. Having communicated with the creature once, perhaps they are attempting to figure a way to do it again. Penelope watches as thirty or so foreign bees head out the window from which the group so recently arrived.

Professor Radigan cannot believe his luck. If only his video camera weren't still in storage, the folks back at the lab would have a howl over this one. He watches as the swarm occupies virtually every cubic foot of his house. Radigan raises his arm gingerly and the hundreds of bees hovering within the vicinity of his hand immediately change their pattern, avoiding contact with his flesh. If only his legs weren't feeling so ticklish, Radigan might be doing a fair imitation of St. Francis of Assisi. Radigan stands in awe of what's taking place about him. Even if Radigan's life could be viewed as being in total jeopardy, a harmony, a tranquility, a cessation of hostility towards all life forms overtakes him.

Brrrriiing.

The swarm inside Radigan's living room does not react well to this abrupt audio intrusion. Radigan sinks his left tooth into his lip as he waits for the bees to calm themselves. The rhythm and order in which they were congregating has been destroyed by the ringing telephone. It's hard for Professor Radigan to focus his eyes on the table where the telephone sits, the agitated bees are darting about so quickly. Radigan doesn't move a muscle. For some reason his legs feel less ticklish.

Penelope hasn't the vaguest idea what's going on. Her body feels like she's flown into a wall at top speed, aided by a strong following wind. She barely has time to recover from the shock of the first ringing assault when it happens again.

Brrrriiing.

-Never should have left the hive. Never should have listened to those guys. If I get out of this place alive, I promise I'll never do anything like this again. -

Penelope definitely isn't having as good a time as she was having a few moments ago. She feels as badly as she did two years ago when some stray dog almost swallowed her. That was a shock to the system. But right now the main concern consists in avoiding midair collisions with a bunch of folks she used to consider friends.

Penelope senses an alien bee may be attempting to get a message out to the rest of the swarm. A degree of calm enters the chaos but Penelope is having too tough a time avoiding collision to understand what the outlander is trying to communicate.

Brrrriiing.

That does it. Penelope collides with one of her former pals from the cell block, three high and two over.

It's a rapid drop. Fortunately for Penelope her fall is slowed by the numerous lesser collisions she keeps incurring during this unelevatored descent.

Penelope's substantially battered orbs behold the foundation precipitously approaching. From the time Penelope first came to consciousness in the hive, her entire existence replays itself. Penelope has never been as bored in her life as she finds herself at the moment, reviewing endless repetitions of hive life. Same cell day after day. Same missions foraging among flowers. Same enforced communality of the hive. As she nears the floor, Penelope reluctantly accepts the cessation of her existence. At least smashing into timelessness won't be routine.

"I'm not home right now."

Shock waves. Again Penelope is beehandled by sound waves and abruptly discovers herself forced in an upward direction. Observing the floor recede, she feels sound waves penetrate her corporeal being. Penelope tries to control her wings but they fail in response to her most rudimentary commands. At least she no longer remains on a collision course with infinity.

"If you leave you're name and number,"

Buffeted by waves from every direction, Penelope no longer can control being thrust against the equally disoriented torsos of her hive mates. Her substantive fear at the moment consists in being stung by a member of her swarm. What a pitiful way for a bee to die. Two bees for that matter. Penelope imagines she's entered a whirlpool which cannot decide whether it's located in the northern or southern hemisphere. She ceases her struggle. Penelope allows fate to do with her as it will. As it already seems to be doing.

"I'll get back to you as soon as I can. Thank you."

Tone.

Maximum turbulence followed by a serenity Zen masters rarely achieve on sabbatical. The swarm, once again acting as a unit, converges with elegant concord towards the answering machine whose now mellifluous tone rekindles within their cadre the spirit of coöperation and interdependence so conspicuously absent moments before.

Silence.

Encircling the black plastic gadget, the swarm awaits an attack from this device, so completely capable of tossing them into any number of hell's circles. As Penelope reorients himself to the tranquility of Radigan's home, she contemplates her relation to the universe at large. Finding none, Penelope feels content maintaining a holding pattern above the answering machine. If the machine isn't there to give answers to Penelope's questions concerning her relation to the universe it certainly should be named something else.

"Please come to the phone, Professor Radigan."

These sounds cause no turbulence. Even Penelope, with limited experience of the human language, understands these phonemes are associated with walking/talking mammal communication. But the words are not of the stupendous volume which engendered the disturbance moments before. As the swarm continues to hover. Professor Radigan strides across the room, picks up the phone's receiver and whispers, "I'm here. Are you who I think you are?"

Outside the house, enveloping a massive post housing a telephone company switch box, one hundred and twenty-eight bees perform a dance never previously witnessed on this planet. Or any planet. With outlander bees directing, this mini-swarm performs a binary two step, choreographed to emulate the Hayes modem configuration. Using 2400 bits per second as a baseline, the bees attain binary emulation of a generic human voice via digital transmission patterns. The outlanders use a Mid-Atlantic American accent, conceding the southwestern drawl they originally hoped to achieve to be somewhat beyond their present mimetic capabilities.

"May we watch television with you?"

This seems a reasonable request to Professor Radigan. Considering the fact that these bees can pretty much demand anything their overworked hearts desire, Radigan considers allowing the swarm to sit by his Sony not so far out of line. Radigan wonders what kind of snacks they enjoy.

"Sure. Anything particular you want to watch?"

There is a silence on the line. Then Professor Radigan discerns sounds similar to those of someone attempting to jump start a Volkswagen beetle when it's ten degrees below zero outside and nobody's changed the oil for six months. After a few seconds the sound harmonizes into a pattern resembling a human voice.

"The Queen, Professor Radigan, we need to see the last queen."

Which takes Radigan somewhat by surprise. But not much. "Any idea what channel."

Again the line goes momentarily silent, then the bees resume in a more assertive manner. "Channel F on your cable tuner, Professor Radigan. And if you'd please hurry, we don't want to miss the opening credits." The connection ceases.

-Prize bunch of insects. First they come to the house virtually uninvited, at least they called first, now they want to speed things up.-

Professor Radigan considers not turning the television on, but decides, scrutinizing the sheer number of his house guests, to let the bees watch whatever they want to watch. Well, probably isn't every day they get to watch cable.

As the bees' away team reenters the cozy confines of Radigan's home, the swarm and their host for this afternoon's telecast settle down for the best American culture has to offer.

DONATION TO SCIENCE

Big Aloysius never even considered donating his body to science. Not while he's living, not when he's dead. There's enough going south in his life without worrying about some deminerd in a lab coat vulturing around while Big Aloysius gasps for that last extra kick of oxygen. Never give yourself the slightest reason to die. Hanging in isn't a walk in the park at the best of times.

Big Aloysius sits in the green room awaiting his call from the stage manager's assistant. The most he ever wanted to do was find Little Aloysius and now with the bees and everything else, Big Aloysius isn't certain this is the best way to conduct his search.

He shouldn't have spoken to the newspapers. And no matter how much money they gave him, he shouldn't have allowed the guy from National Public Radio the right to act as his exclusive agent. Some kid smack out of college. Big Aloysius is confident anyone with an I.Q. over fifty would have negotiated a better contract than the one Big Aloysius is saddled with for the next two years. Big Aloysius doesn't consider network cable at present to be a concept who's time has come.

And the hairdresser. Big Aloysius shouldn't have allowed it. The last fashion statement he made was in the early 1970's and he always thought bearing a distant resemblance to General George Armstrong Custer should be good enough for anyone. Now Big Aloysius looks like an extremely tense rooster who's strolled onto the wrong high voltage wires. It isn't even his natural color. No more of this. Fire the agent and next time around make sure the contract specifically forbids messing with his natural image. A man has to get some respect.

Along with Big Aloysius in the green room sit people one might consider to be the ultimate dregs of society. Fortunately, the geek with the glasses is the first out of there. Big Aloysius can't remember ever seeing anyone so fidgety. And he kept inspecting the kitchen utensils and pots and pans. Maybe he thought someone was out to poison him with his own food. The green room feels a lot calmer since the fidgety one's departure.

In one corner of the green room sits a foreign jerk who keeps leaping to his feet every three minutes as if he were being subjected to a military snap inspection. He stands up, clicks his heels, spins around then takes his seat again. Stand up, click, spin around, click, sit. If he picked a bale of cotton Big Aloysius might have understood what this fruitcake was doing.

The remaining guest appears to be one of those wackos who imagines they're invisible to everyone else. He's wrapped in a blanket sitting in the corner of the room where they keep the ancient magazines. He isn't doing much of anything but now and then some words come from over his way which sound like a language not necessarily English. When the stage manager's assistant comes into the room she speaks with everyone except the guy in the corner with the cape. Big Aloysius will be extremely happy when they finally get around to him and he can get the hell out of this zoo.

And eventually they do. Opening the door a crack, the stage manager's assistant whispers Big Aloysius's name. **IT'S SHOWTIME!** Big Aloysius rises from his chair and for the first time since the bees attacked the driver's rig, Big Aloysius becomes aware of adrenalin surging through his body. The vein on the left side of his neck pumps to a beat mimicking the worst heavy metal riff ever recorded and his forehead feels like it's preceding his body by roughly two hundred yards. Big Aloysius has never had stage fright before but then again, Big Aloysius has never before been on stage.

Eventually the stage manager's assistant comes over to where Big Aloysius is standing as if nailed to the floor by fifteen non-union, illegal alien, Swedish carpenters, and taking him by the hand leads him out the door. Immediately adjoining the green room is a backstage waiting area and Big Aloysius, spotting a large red exit sign, pauses momentarily in revery of exodus. But the stage manager's assistant, supremely accustomed to flop sweatitis in its unlimited shapes and forms, gently nudges Big Aloysius. Pausing as they approach the curtain, she waits for the proper cue before abruptly shoving Big Aloysius onto the stage. The light from two arc lamps hit Big Aloysius right between the eyes and for the first four seconds of his onstage career, Big Aloysius is another member of the walking/talking unconscious.

PROPER SNACKS

Radigan hasn't a clue how to properly entertain his guests. They seem content enough, resting their haunches on any seemingly satisfying surface, but the historic nature of this afternoon's visit distresses Radigan's mind.

What exactly is the proper snack to serve guests in this most awkward portion of the afternoon when it's too late for lunch and too early for cocktails? Radigan wonders if he should whip up a batch of stingers but scratches the idea, conjuring up the image of a house overflowing with besotted bees. It's not a pretty picture.

They seem content. Radigan stands staring at the television, puzzling over what to do next. A disgruntled hum emerges from behind him and Professor Radigan realizes he's blocking the view of a hundred or so of his guests. He moves towards the couch and a throng of bees parked there create a mini-blizzard as they make enough room for Radigan to sit.

Penelope doesn't know what to make of any of this. When she awoke this morning, the outlanders promised a day full of rare excitement and the possibility of better lives for all the bees in the hive. Penelope knows seventy percent of what the outlanders are saying is nonsense but she figures she didn't have much else planned for the afternoon, so, what the hell.

Penelope attempts focusing upon the grey rectangular area where the outlander bees have directed the swarms collected vision. There are sounds emanating from the rectangle and Penelope recognizes the patterns as those of walking/talking mammal speech. Fortunately, their host has lowered the volume to a whisper and Penelope is lulled into a perching somnambulation primarily induced by theme music as it frequently interrupts the walking/talking mammal voices.

Penelope focuses on the television screen, a visual pattern begins to emerge from the scattered electrical impulses. The outlanders told the swarm they would soon need to know how to interpret images in two dimensions rather than the five to which they have grown accustomed. As the swarm settles in for some afternoon T.V.. Penelope opens her mind to the new experience. There is nothing to fear but ignorance and Penelope knows the best way to learn something new is not to fight it. Perhaps the humans know something bees don't. Penelope doubts it but is willing to give them time to present their case.

TUBES

Big Aloysius never wanted to be on television. Big Aloysius never wanted to be anywhere but in his own woods with Little Aloysius beside him. The reason he's in this television studio is his hope that someone will hear the story he has to tell and assist him in his seemingly endless search for his beloved dog. Big Aloysius doesn't want to talk about any bees. Big Aloysius prays he hasn't made a big mistake.

The compact human entity seems to know Big Aloysius even before Imelda introduces them in front of the live studio audience consisting mostly of former members of the President for Life (Unless There's a Massive Breakthrough in Cryogenics) of the Philippines and Surrounding Suburbs, What's-his-name's palace guard and their families, along with executives from the cable network's parent company and citizens picked up from the street who are more than happy to be entombed within the warm confines of a television studio.

The bees aren't enjoying the show much, at least that's the impression Professor Radigan gets sitting among them. He tries to guess their emotions by reading their body language and overall noise level.

The bees go berserk when the camera takes a closeup of Imelda asking Big Aloysius one of the deeply thought provoking questions for which she will soon become transcontinentally famous. Suddenly, Professor Radigan is in the midst of a swarm of bees who insist on buzzing the room even though their air traffic controllers are obviously still walking the picket line. This time around Radigan is under attack. Bees hurl into him at tremendous speeds. The television set appears to be under an even more hostile assault. Professor Radigan hasn't a clue what to do. He tries remaining calm. It's as good a choice as any at the moment.

Penelope is confused. Having only moments before begun to understand the electronic patterns on the gray screen were meant to signify humans performing various behaviors, Penelope is horrified when the first image she perceives is the electronic representation of the hive's greatest enemy. She buzzes the room, attempting to dissipate the heat building up within her body as powerful emotions come to a boiling point within her. Penelope has time to think since avoiding collision is out of the question given prevailing conditions.

-The outlander bees were correct in everything they said. How is it an entire population can intrinsically be aware of various facts but never truly come to terms with them until someone from outside the community brings them to the forefront? How could the hive have continued its existence assuming their enemy remained far distant? How could they have been so complacent, so easily lulled into lives as simple hunter gatherers? Where was the communal wisdom of which her tribe was so proud? How could they have let this mortal enemy get control of a communication medium vital to walking/talking mammal existence?-

Where are the thoughts Penelope is having at the moment coming from? Penelope is flabbergasted by her own analysis. There must be something in the air.

GREAT PICTURE

Big Aloysius doesn't particularly appreciate the woman who is interrogating him about the bees. Big Aloysius hasn't had the chance to show anyone his photograph of Little Aloysius. It's a great picture, Big Aloysius and Little Aloysius took it together in a drug store when Big Aloysius went into town to get Little Aloysius a new collar so Big Aloysius could hang from this collar the tags he'd made sure to get so he and Little Aloysius could never be legally separated. It's a great picture and there are three others on the strip almost as good.

The compact human entity is having a marvelous time. Other than needing to play up to her co-host, there isn't anything else she could desire. At first she thought she might have some trouble reading dialogue from cue cards but after the director gave her a few tips, she feels completely at ease whenever she has to glance to the cards in order to say something clever and spontaneous to her co-host or one of their very special guests.

This certainly is one of the compact human entity's many dreams come true. Of course the compact human entity cannot recall ever having this particular dream, but there is no denying this is a dream come true. The only things the compact human entity ever wanted were a house in the country, a garden, a cat, and the rest of the little things which go with a dream well within the compact human entity's conception of the plausible. A man who loves her would be an extra bonus. Maybe two or three even more compact human entities playing in the yard. Simple dreams like owning a home with a kitchen and a working range hood overshadowing the microwave-conventional oven.

This is nice. Since the compact human entity arrived to work the show, everyone she's met has impressed her with their attitude. Their attitude being if there is anything the compact human entity needs or wants, one of them will be more than happy to take care of the task. It's been a long time since she's been used to people doing nice things for her. The compact human entity finds this exceedingly nice.

WORRIED, WORRIED, WORRIED

The compact human entity was worried the first time she met Imelda Marcos, former wife of the President for Life (Unless There's a Massive Breakthrough in Cryogenics) of the Philippines and Surrounding Suburbs, What's-his-name, and celebrity in her own rite. What is a compact human entity lik
e herself doing on a national cable television show with as big a star as Imelda Marcos? Good question. Let's try to answer this one.

The compact human entity often wonders what would happen if one night, while walking in the woods all by herself, a hovering humongous spaceship came into her line of sight, landed, and two aliens emerged from the ship to kidnap her. She wonders about this still.

But this has nothing to do with the reason why the compact human entity is on national cable television. Why she is on national cable television has a lot to do with what happened to the compact human entity after she left Los Angeles. Let's simply say the compact human entity left Los Angeles and leave the reasons why she left Los Angeles to historians.

The car is travelling at approximately eighty-five miles per hour. This isn't an excessive speed when travelling cross-country. The compact human entity has been on the road over two days and now she cruises through a piece of land which may be the most peculiar portion of the country she's ever seen.

A group of people were forced to immigrate into this part of the country because no other place would let them stay. The compact human entity imagines their coming upon this endless sea of waste. Salt flats. Sure. Godforsaken wilderness would certainly be preferable to this particular patch of real estate. The compact human entity drives along wishing she were anywhere else.

She pulls her car into a rest stop by the side of the interstate wondering if the few cars she sees sporting local license plates carry descendants of the original pioneers. The compact human entity wonders if they will ever be capable of forgiving their ancestors for stranding them in this dump. No wonder uncounted thousands of them take federal jobs and proceed to mark the government with their own uniquely bent view of the universe. It must be nice being the President of the United States of America and Points South and be surrounded by gun toting fanatic cowboys who know if they mess up they'll be sent back to a land where for miles on end the only sight you can see is salt. The compact human entity wonders if the total number of heart attacks in this state is higher than the national average.

The compact human entity walks to the rear of the rest station and looks towards the horizon. There is a nothingness here like nothing she's previously experienced. It's as if she's standing in the middle of a beach without the sea breeze and without any water in the ocean. Sand clings to itself for companionship. The compact human entity sits on a bench scarred by its life of exposure to wind blown salt. She is far from where she started, too far to turn back.

She has an even longer way to go. And surrounding her is sun and salt. The only humans she sees would undoubtedly enjoy her being another number in a harem. Why in the world do people live in such an inhospitable place?

She could end it all here and no one would know. Expending minimum effort, she could toss her identification papers into the roadside litter container and stroll out onto the sea of salt. It would be a dry, horrible death. Such thoughts keep her going.

Returning to her car, the compact human entity drives another hour. Pulling off the interstate, she enters what passes for a town in this part of the country. Spotting a joint she thinks might be a reasonably respectable eatery,
she pulls into the parking lot. Life is a gamble and chancing where to eat while on the road is the biggest risk many people ever need take.

From the look's of the restaurant's interior the compact human entity might as well be in any town anywhere. The compact human entity might be having a vision from her childhood or she could as easily be seeing her future. If she closes her eyes there is no way for her to describe what she has seen seconds before. Her mental picture blurs with the too many similar restaurants she's experienced in her brief life. Restaurant Design 101.

There are more of the same people surrounding her. The compact human entity finds a booth where she can see all the activities of the place while at the same time keep her back to the wall. Why she needs the security of a wall at her back, she doesn't know. The only thing the compact human entity knows is that she doesn't feel comfortable in this insignificant restaurant amid a sea of salt.

A waitress approaches her booth and the compact human entity gives her an order which wouldn't strain the intelligence of a gnat working tables its first day. The waitress asks the compact human entity to repeat her order. The compact human entity repeats the order in as clear and as loud a voice as she can manage without attracting undue attention. The waitress looks the compact human entity straight in the face and once again asks the compact human entity for her order. The compact human entity stares into the eyes of the waitress, and in as loud and as distinct a voice as she can produce, gives the postally deaf waitress the order.

"I'd like a cup of coffee and a grilled cheese sandwich. Please."

Which is as loud as and as distinct as the compact human entity can get short of screaming. The waitress stares at the compact human entity with an expression usually reserved for puppies who have shown they are not yet qualified for the great indoors.

"Honey, if you want something, order it. Or, you'll have to leave. You think about it. I'll be back in a couple of minutes."

The compact human entity wonders if so much salt in the locals' diet has produced chronic hearing loss. Twisting her body in the booth, she tries to get the attention of a gentleman reading the local paper in an adjoining booth.

"Excuse me, sir. Did you hear what the waitress said to me?"

Which is an innocuous enough question for anyone parked in a seat at a cheap restaurant in the middle of the largest amount of spilt salt anyone has ever encountered. But the guy doesn't look up from his funnies.

The compact human entity hears the theme from "The Twilight Zone" play in her head. This is not the reaction the compact human entity is used to having when she orders lunch. Opening her bag, the compact human entity takes out a pocket mirror and watches her lips as she murmurs softly to herself.

"This is one of the most ridiculous situations I've ever been in."

Her lips are moving and the audio checks out. The waitress returns to the booth.

"You ready now, honey, or you want to sit here for all day and waste everybody's time?" The waitress applies pen to pad, ready for action.

"Thank you, miss, I'll have a cup of tea and a lettuce and tomato sandwich." The compact human entity changes her order in case the miscommunication is being caused by a simple case of harmonic distortion.

"Honey, if you're going to fool around, I'll ask you to leave."

Which at this point is fine with the compact human entity. The compact human entity is about to tell off the waitress when she realizes her comments probably won't do any good at all. Rising from her booth, the compact human entity gives the waitress the most irate glare she can muster from her none too complete repertoire of irate glares and abandons the restaurant.

On the street the compact human entity doesn't have a great deal of time to ponder the incident. The car she drove from Los Angeles to this step down from a godforsaken wilderness has its front end in the air and is being hoisted into position by a police tow truck. Running towards her car the compact human entity screams as loud as she can, but her pleas, as in every tow job since the dawn of Ford and mass marketing, fall upon disregarding ears.

As the tow truck pulls into traffic, dangling the catch of the day from its tail, the compact human entity spots a motorcycle cop perched on its bike, ready to flee the scene of the crime.

Catching up to the cop, the compact human entity grabs the officer by the arm screaming, "Hey, what you doing with my car?"

Which means nothing to the cop. The cop does react to being assaulted by someone who is so obviously an out-of-towner. Fortunately for the compact human entity, the officer recently has been trained not to shoot first and request proof of age later.

"You got a problem?" This being the sum total of the officer's witty repartee.

The compact human entity doesn't know what to say next. Most of her life has been spent trying hard not to get the attention of police and finding herself in a situation where she needs it is truly a novel experience.

Not wishing to go through the entire dumb act again, suffice it to say the compact human entity is as equally unable to communicate her thoughts to the officer as she was in getting across her lunch order to the waitress. After waving her arms about, stomping her foot two or three times, and causing as much of a scene as one can when none of the words one uses seem to register with the intended audience, the officer calls for a squad car as backup. After waiting seven minutes for the officer's backup to arrive, the compact human entity is escorted to the local cop shop.

At the cop shop the compact human entity gets possession of paper and pencil and begins writing to her captors in words she is certain they will understand. Wrong. Another case of faulty logic on the part of the compact human entity. Since the restaurant, she has become convinced there is something drastically wrong with her ability to communicate ideas through speech. Now that she can write down her complaints and comments, she is equally confident communication will be established. Still wrong.

Police officers of various shapes, sizes and genders ignore the written word of the compact human entity. Now all this is a bit too too, even for a stranger from out of town who's never seen a hunk of barren wasteland like the one surrounding this town.

As the desk sergeant takes down the statement of the arresting officer, the compact human entity listens, becoming moderately catatonic on hearing the officer's version of events.

"Parked in a disabled zone. No sticker. Called Charlie. Towed away. Then, when I'm getting back on my bike, she grabs my arm and steps on my foot. Doesn't apologize or nothing. Starts screaming at me in some gibberish I've never heard before in my life. Had to call up backup to bring her in. Book her on interfering with a police officer carrying out the law.

"Stopped in at Rita's diner and Roberta she says she was in the place jabbering like no tomorrow and left without a tip. They might want to press charges later. Judge Willoughby says she upset his lunch with her shouting and making a fuss. Disturbing the peace will do, but you'll have to get a statement from the Judge."

The compact human entity doesn't know what to make of the officer's complaint. She understands the cop is understandably puffing up the facts to make the case, but the compact human entity doesn't understand what the officer is talking about when the officer says she's speaking a language the officer's never heard before. The compact human entity has spoken English her entire life and that's the language everyone else is speaking.

The police take the compact human entity's handbag from her and examine the contents. She recognizes the items: mostly junk and makeup from her past, but the compact human entity pays particular attention to her wallet which contains necessary identification, as well as credit cards.

"Isn't carrying identification." The sergeant makes this statement in such a matter of fact way the compact human entity doesn't grasp its significance. The two lawmen ignore the compact human entity's wallet and carefully examine everything else in the bag. As the arresting officer breaks apart her lipstick, conducting what the compact human entity assumes is a drug search, the compact human entity launches into another of her tirades.

"I don't know what the two of you are playing at, but let me tell you right now, you aren't getting away with it.   The two cops glare at the compact human entity with a mixture of bewilderment and contempt as if the words are meaningless to them but the volume is painful to their ears.

Sitting in her cell, the compact human entity wonders how in the world she ended up in such a predicament. She spends her life in as nice a way as she can, and never goes out of her way to hurt anybody or anything. Now she sits in a jail cell in a part of the country where she's never been before and nobody seems to comprehend what she's trying to say. They act as if she's speaking a foreign language. It's a tad confusing.

It's as if she ceased to exist. But that's not right. The compact human entity feels the same way she has always felt. She can't be speaking a foreign language. The compact human entity checks her pulse. The same as it always is give or take a bit of anxiety which might speed it up a smidgen. The compact human entity knows she isn't dead, as she's always understood death, so the answer lies elsewhere.

The compact human entity listens to sounds emerging from other occupants of the building. She examines snatches of overheard conversation for any clue as to why she's in the predicament in which she finds herself. Nothing. A few of the phrases increase her moderate paranoia but she discards them as being what they are, overheard snatches of conversation having no true bearing on herself or her situation. Or at least that's what she hopes. The compact human entity hopes they aren't talking about her. She doesn't know anymore.

A jailor in a different colored uniform walks by her cell and nods as if to say everything is all right and will continue the same as long as the compact human entity maintains her calm and doesn't start shouting. The compact human entity assumes she is meant to be calmed by this human presence. She is. But only by the most minuscule amount. She realizes she's being tossed a crumb.

Waking from a short nap the compact human entity sees three male civilians looking across the bars into her cell. Not being totally awake, the compact human entity at first cannot understand what the three are whispering. As consciousness reasserts itself, the compact human entity realizes she may be in trouble.

SHADRACH Too skinny.

MESHACH Too skinny for real life, but, maybe not for a special.

ABEDNEGO (Grunts.)

SHADRACH Want my opinion, send her to the mountains. Shortage for the past few years. Tired listening their bellyaching.

MESHACH Too fine an item for up there. She wouldn't last long enough.

ABEDNEGO Hurry up, will you.

MESHACH There's no need to rush. People make mistakes that way.

SHADRACH Find her people. Want make sure no slips. Slips cost money. Why we're here.

MESHACH The investigation is in progress but I've been assured there's a ninety-five percent chance she will satisfy our needs. We have the time to wait.

We should find out if she has marketable special abilities.

ABEDNEGO Talents. Not nowadays. Two of mine can't even sew.

The compact human entity isn't following any of this. "Can you people help me? Nobody seems to know what I'm talking about."

The three men stare through the bars. Standing behind Meshach, Abednego seemingly takes the compact human entity's meaning.

ABEDNEGO Special talents? Never seen any myself.

SHADRACH New markets. New markets, new men, new requirements. New cash.

MESHACH Let's go. We'll discuss this over lunch.

The compact human entity falls back to sleep. When she awakens the sun which once brightly illuminated her cell now informs her hours have passed. On a short table next to her cot is a glass of water and an orange. Nothing else in the cell appears to have changed. She drinks half the water, peels the orange and slowly savors separate sections as the dim sun fades to darkness.

The jailhouse remains quiet. The compact human entity finds the building's silence more disturbing than the reality of her being in jail. With the loss of light the compact human entity can only lay on her cot and wait. What she awaits, she does not know.

With morning light, the building's sounds awaken the compact human entity. Next to her cot are another glass of water and another orange. Completing her toilet, the compact human entity lies back and indifferently consumes her breakfast. No one comes near her cell for the entire day.

Two mornings later, the compact human entity's third day in captivity, the three men once again appear outside her cell as she regains consciousness after an afternoon nap. The compact human entity decides against attempting communication and waits quietly in her cell until one of the men speaks directly to her.

MESHACH   Do you have any special abilities?

The compact human entity hardly knows how to answer this question. - What does he mean by "special abilities"? Don't they know they won't be able to understand anything even if I do speak? Why are they keeping me locked up like this? - There are too many questions colliding with one another within the compact human entity's mind for her to answer the stranger.

SHADRACH Useless. To mountains. Not what they want. Special. Not special at all. Enough.
ABEDNEGO Let's not waste any more time.
MESHACH   We'll give her some real food today and see what happens. We've seen reactions like this before. A little time, a little consideration and she'll open up. We're dealing with a human entity here.

And the three men walk away. As the outer door closes, the compact human entity whispers, "Yes."

Later in the day, as the compact human entity continues her enforced rest on her cot, the same jailor who came by the first day comes to a stop outside her cell. The jailor opens the cell door but motions the compact human entity to stay where she is when she attempts to get up. He places a bowl of soup, some crackers and a glass of milk on the table. Closing and locking the cell door behind him, the jailor smiles at the compact human entity. The compact human entity stares at the back of his retreating head as the outer door locks shut.

If not tasty, at least the soup nourishes. The milk is superb. The compact human entity takes another nap as the meal slowly digests in her stomach.

The compact human entity opens her eyes to the ¼ light of what she assumes to be a truck of some sort. Possibly an ambulance since she is strapped to what seems to be a stretcher. She rides along flat on her back for what must be hours. The compact human entity drifts in and out of her slumbers, each time awakening to the darkness and motion.

MESHACH   She should sleep for the rest of the ride.

SHADRACH   Special talent.

MESHACH   It's not for us to say. They came up with something.

SHADRACH   Deliver. We deliver. Nobody else. Crazy.

MESHACH   Not for us to say. Strangers are necessary for the prosperity of the people. Not for us to say if the elders order us to deliver this woman somewhere. Not for any of us to say.

SHADRACH   Ride around. All night. For nothing. Wrong.

ABEDNEGO Will you two keep quiet. Somebody's got to drive this rig. Two of you jabbering the whole time doesn't make my life any easier.

In the morning the compact human entity awakens as the men unstrap her from the stretcher. An undiffused sun blinds her eyes. The clear, cool air bites her skin. She recognizes nearby birdsong. The three men escort her into a large estate house. A metallic taste lingers in her mouth.

"What a charming compact human entity you are. Yes, you are. I will tell you this right now. Right this very instant before you even have the chance to take off your coat and have some of this lovely tea I've only just now for you made. Only just now for you with my very hands. Yes, I have. Yes, I have. Only just now for you with my very hands I have made for you this tea."

The compact human entity doesn't know what to make of this onslaught of congeniality. From what her blurred vision reveals to her, there appears to be a short woman standing directly ahead with what might be a cup and saucer extended from her right hand. As the men release their holds on the compact human entity, the sudden lack of restraints causes her to lose balance. She recovers in a moment but on attempting to take off her coat, the compact human entity realizes she isn't wearing one, only the clothes she's worn since before the police locked her up. The compact human entity doesn't know how many days it's been but the scent emanating from her ensemble reveal it's been at the least a couple of days.

"You must come into my fine new house and make yourself to comfortable. Oh, what an ordeal must you have gone through. I, myself, no I, myself, would not the strength you have. No. No. A brave compact human entity what you are. Yes, you are. Please, follow me and into my parlor come and sit and have some fine, very fine tea."

The compact human entity can't think of anything else to do, so as the short woman takes her by the arm, the compact human entity allows herself to be escorted to a massive and undeniably quite comfortable couch where she rests her abused body while sipping some fine, very fine tea, the name of which the compact human entity wouldn't be able to tell you if her life depended on it.

"You poor, poor compact human entity. I know how horrible these last days must for you have been. Nobody who knew about what you were saying anything. No friends. Alone without anyone to offer you sympathy the slightest bit of. I know how you must felt. I've been through situations similar. I have, yes. I have been through situations which make what you have been through seem like a walk in the park on a beautiful summer evening when the wind is gently blowing and you know it soon will rain but it won't rain too soon, so you have time to stroll to a lovely restaurant where the man on your arm pulls out your chair for you and behaves the way are meant to behave gentlemen. Yes, I have been through situations which make your situation look like a in the park stroll."

The compact human entity nobly maintains her perfect posture and pose of rapt attention as the short woman speaks, but soon even the compact human entity's posture gives in to her bewilderment. She was shanghaied days ago, and now this woman is prattling away as if nothing happened. Well, nothing happened to the short woman, but the compact human entity knows she's been through hell and she isn't about to forget the whole thing even if the short woman makes the best tea in the entire known universe. Somebody is going to pay for her pain. Whether or not it's the woman sitting across the room or not is still to be decided but the compact human entity knows for a certainty someone is going to pay.

Then the compact human entity comes to a realization she would have paid every cent she possessed not to have realized. The compact human entity, with eyes rapidly adjusting to changing light, recognizes her hostess. The compact human entity sits on the sofa and realizes exactly with whom she is sharing a cup of tea. Her hostess is none other than the dragon lady of the Philippines and Surrounding Suburbs, the lady mistress executioner herself, the soon to be national cable daytime talk show hostess for the entire U.S. of A.P.S., the possessor of the daintiest pedal digits this side of the equator, the former etiquette teacher to Ron and Nancy, the indomitable, the irrepressible, the spontaneous, the living and the quick, Imelda Marcos!

Shit.

Which should explain everything to the compact human entity but doesn't come close. Her recognition makes the situation more confusing since a personage such as the one she has only recently recognized comes with far more baggage (both ways) than an ordinary abductor would consider appropriate for transport (both ways).

The compact human entity is aware she should be happy she isn't dead. She is. She does, however, wonder how long this particular form of incarnation will last. The compact human entity understands she no longer exists in the land of the merely deranged, she has entered the territory of powerful wackos, and escape from this zone of existence is extremely infrequent. It must be extremely infrequent since the compact human entity has never heard of anyone who's done it. Sipping her tea the compact human entity realizes sooner or later she will become one of these wackos or the odds of her surviving will diminish appreciably. This is not the way she planned to spend her weekend.

"You have finished the tea for you I made? Yes? Good for now is the time for you and I to talk about the many, many interesting things to talk about we have.

"You see, you were not brought here because my three friends who brought you here nothing else had to do. No. This is not a true in the least fact. They have many, many matters to attend and their time not inexpensive is. No, not inexpensive at all it is. It is much too expensive for most people to have men like the three who brought you here for them doing odd work. They ain't cheap, no."

So far the compact human entity isn't making head nor tail of what this illustrious old matriarch is talking about. But as long as she's talking the compact human entity isn't having anything even more horrible occur to her. One point for the good guys.

"Wouldn't you on television like to appear like other important people in this country? Yes, wouldn't you, you would? You can say you wouldn't but know I you would. No, you cannot fool me even as your face I see you wish you could."

By this point the compact human entity is fed up to her armpits. Since before the first day of her captivity the compact human entity hasn't uttered a syllable understood by anyone. Now she has the former first lady of the Philippines and Surrounding Suburbs sitting only a few feet from her, a ready and seemingly willing audience for her tale of tribulation, but the compact human entity cannot bring to mind a single word to utter. After days of drug like captivity, with this chance of seeking retribution, with a light at the end of her tunnel, the compact human entity cannot verbalize.

Part of the problem centers on the compact human entity's inability to decide whether Imelda Marcos of the Philippines and Surrounding Suburbs is her captor or her liberator. But, as has been said myriad times, a job is a job.

"You liked my résumé. I'm glad. But don't you think your way of interviewing someone is somewhat eccentric?" At last the compact human entity is able to say something. She'd had a few jobs in her career, however, the recruiting tactics of this organization seem downright odd. But the compact human entity needs the job, so what the hey.

"You so right are, my friend, you so very, very right are. It was not I who decided our acquaintance should make this way. No, you it was. No need you for learn Tagalog. It most, most beautiful on your part thought, but my dear, friend dear, it not necessary. We only broadcast within the United States of America and Points South."

And then realization dawns stunningly upon the compact human entity. There was a reason why everyone she met the last few days didn't understand a word she said. If she listened to tapes of herself from that period, the compact human entity probably wouldn't understand her speech herself. And they say you can't prepare too much for a job interview.

As soon as the compact human entity saw the ad in the "Hollywood Redundant" she knew she had to have the job. Imelda Marcos, former first lady of the Philippines and Surrounding Suburbs, has been her idol since the compact human entity was a child. How could the compact human entity not answer an ad seeking a co-host for a famous wife of a famous deposed leader, who needs someone with American warmth and vitality to offset the charismatic, slightly oriental, charms of the hostess. The compact human entity knew exactly who the hostess would be and had a résumé, along with pictures and video tape, in the overnight mail within an hour. Within two hours the compact human entity was packing to leave Los Angeles for New York. She purchased "Tagalog in Seven Lessons" cassettes and "Tagalog Letters for All

Occasions" and by the end of the week was in her car driving east with her Tagalog language tapes blaring from the car stereo as they'd been blaring on her apartment stereo since she purchased them.

And that's what must have happened. Having been on the road for over thirty-six hours with only a few hours spent in a Motel 8½, to recharge her own batteries as well as those of the Walkman she played continually while she slept, the compact human entity achieved osmotic parity with the Tagalog language and did not realize she was using Tagalog on the people of the town when she thought she was speaking and writing English.

Learning the language was the extra yard which would put the compact human entity over the top in her interview with Imelda Marcos. The compact human entity never doubted for a millisecond she would be granted an interview. After all, she is the daughter of a past Vice-President of the United States and Points South and this along with her previous media experience and two years hosting the night owl show on the weather channel should have been enough to impress the wife of an ousted dictator, even if Imelda Marcos, the former first lady of the Philippines and Surrounding Suburbs, who had been her idol since she was a much more compact human entity and while on a vice-presidential visit, the former first lady of the Philippines and Surrounding Suburbs had the most wonderful General Oscar de Laleesa lead the compact human entity on an individual, three hour, guided tour of the closets.

They certainly were wonderful closets especially to a compact human entity who as a precocious preteen couldn't see the dust collecting on top of the garments hanging there. Scheduled for the next day was a special showing of the shoe collections but, unfortunately, the compact human entity's visit was cut short when the Vice-President of the United States and Points South was obliged to return to Washington in order to appoint a new Secretary of the Interior since the present Secretary of the Interior had been apprehended, in flagrante delicto, with a permanent exhibit at the Washington zoo. But that's the past and this is the present.

WHERE'S MY WALLET?

The Ghost of Pope John Paul I can't find his wallet anywhere. He's searched the house completely, and even after searching the waste paper baskets, he's produced no results worth mentioning. The problem is the Ghost of Pope John Paul I can't remember the last time he had his wallet, so backtracking to where he might have lost track of it is impossible.

-Never should have let her out on probation. I never will learn. People too often revert to previous criminal behaviors even after you show them a better way. They can maintain a new personality for an extended period of time then suddenly snap back into their old ways.-

The Ghost of Pope John Paul I is a classic example of "fool me twice, shame on me."

This is not to say The Ghost of Pope John Paul I is anything remotely resembling a fool. Even if the money in his wallet is long gone. The Ghost of Pope John Paul I is seeking his billfold mostly for identification purposes. He never had enough media exposure to be instantly recognizable on the street the way the rest of his late twentieth century brethren are. The wallet helps him gain entrance into various places. It's similar to being proofed at a bar.

-Should write an article on the subject of showing more kindness and generosity to the post-quick. Might lead to a revival of my earlier writings. Beethoven consistently manages to scare up new scores when he feels like it, even if he never tells anyone exactly how he does it. He still won't listen to anyone. Astral geniuses should be avoided.-

The Ghost of Pope John Paul I rearranges a couple of cushions on the couch and lies down, remembering to remove his shoes first.

-Too much work to do and so confining a time frame. If she took my wallet she's in more trouble than she can imagine. Lightfingering a spirit's billfold. The nerve of these animates. Time for a nap and get the old thoughts together.-

Now some of you may be thinking, "Hey, this is no way for the Ghost of Pope John Paul I to act! This isn't the way any ghost acts. I know, I've read the literature."

This is a valid complaint. More to the point, many of you undoubtedly don't believe in the existence of ghosts. (We'll skip any discussions of Paracletes or super budgies for the moment.)

Ghosts are what they are. Indefinable existences who show up when you least expect them. Or when you most expect them which also means when you least expect them since if they sometimes show up when you least expect them and sometimes show up when you most expect them, they fall into the range of the most unpredictable, so no matter when you expect them they'll show up when you least expect them even if you expect them every conscious minute.

But the Ghost of Pope John Paul I doesn't fall into this category. The Ghost of Pope John Paul I falls into the category of ghost who, if you know he's going to be around at all, is around all the time. You expect him around and he's around. He's a most unpredictable ghost in that when you expect him around, he's there. For ghosts this constitutes significantly unpredictable behavior.

Even the Ghost of Pope John Paul I doesn't remember exactly when or why he was given the assignment he's performing at the moment. It's a relief for ghosts that their memories are completely unreliable or they would continually haunt the places they thought were neat while they were among the quick. The problem is a long time ago ghosts had better memories and they constantly were hanging around the beaches and parks they hung around when they were teenagers, reliving the good old days. Ghost memories were modified, erasing most quick recollections, and now ghosts are considered some of the more diligent workers in the astral force since the only subject their altered memories can readily focus upon is the job at hand. But they do tend to forget everyday necessities as well, which is possibly how the Ghost of Pope John Paul I misplaced his wallet.

Or it may be stolen. As the Ghost of Pope John Paul I endeavors to get in a few "Z"ees on the couch, his mind drifts into the background of his assigned case.

For most of the astral work force, assignments have been distributed on a strict seniority basis since the recertification of their union. Depending upon the amount of time one has hung around the afterwards, you might easily be sent to any number of the various rings of purgatory (hell having been written out of the contract following a massive strike in 1876) to cool your heels for a couple of decades. For one with such a short amount of time in residence within the even greater beyond, it's unusual for the Ghost of Pope John Paul I to receive an assignment at all. Most spirits are considered rookies well into their second century upstairs, but considering his quick résumé, the Ghost of Pope John Paul I was chosen ahead of many with vaster seniority.

The Ghost of Pope John Paul I is certain there will be a review by the Union Board when he returns - at the least he expects a thorough tongue lashing from the shop steward - but the Ghost of Pope John Paul I, in the same manner as his quick self, takes orders when he gets them. He doesn't consider his vows any less binding in this present form, a belief which may lead to future entanglements with his solidarity committee later in his career.

The Ghost of Pope John Paul I searches his pre-nap consciousness for the exact instructions given him before taking this assignment. He knows he has to chaperon a certain woman who was formerly almost a head of state, but he can't remember exactly why it's imperative that he alone be on the case. He distinctly remembers the dispatcher quoting his superiors in saying they wanted the Ghost of Pope John Paul I on the job, but the Ghost of Pope John Paul I cannot remember exactly why they chose him. As he drifts to sleep, fragments of memory repel each other like similar magnetic poles.

White smoke rising from the chimney. Standing in the streets, an entire city watches. The world awaits, standing before Amana Cool Flame ranges as they cook sauce for family dinners and stare at televisions to see if finally, after many, many votes, the new chairman of the board, the C.E.O., the big honcho, has been selected.

In his dream the Ghost of Pope John Paul I sees the people of his flock gather before him. He doesn't view them as an undifferentiated mass but he sees each as the individual they are. They are his friends. He will lead where none before dared to proceed.

Dreamily the Ghost of Pope John Paul I meets and visits his many people. *No, I am not apart from you. I am one of you. There is no need for centralization of wealth. The Church draws its power, like any good union, from the strength of its members and not from any amount of cash, negotiable securities, or real estate available to us. This is not strength. This is attempting to beat the devil at his own game. If finances become a consideration, everything is lost. The battle must be won in the hearts and mind of each individual. By each individual.*

The Ghost of Pope John Paul I dreams of his first dinner at his new place of residence. Food tastes a little off but the Ghost of Pope John Paul I blames it on his emotional state, owing to the recent changes in his life.

On awakening, a mode of being the Ghost of Pope John Paul I realizes doesn't carry quite the same weight it once did - his goals feel much more defined. He'd been a fool when quick and is now being given the opportunity to make up for one or two of his past mistakes. The game is afoot. It has been decided the only man for the job is the Ghost of Pope John Paul I. Fool me once.

But why? There surely were more than enough disreputable quick people hanging around the earth that one or two more couldn't make the slightest difference in the overall omnipresent scheme of things. Why make a fuss about the wife of a second rate dictator from a country which most people consider second rate in and of itself? The Ghost of Pope John Paul I wishes he could remember the exact instructions he was given. But wishes aren't horses so he has to find his wallet if he's going to catch up with his charge.

Got it! Must have been the odd dog. Always nice to have an odd dog around the house but the last time the Ghost of Pope John

Paul I came into the kitchen, Ms. Marcos seemed unduly preoccupied with a large mutt who'd strolled into the kitchen from the garden.

The Ghost of Pope John Paul I knows Imelda Marcos would never be so brazen as to lift the wallet of her parole officer, so taking this into account he searched the entire house from top to bottom, including serious attention being paid to the molecular structure of the furniture, and he concludes the mutt must be the felon. Great, now he knows who did it, but this doesn't explain why or what he's going to do to catch up with both his parolee and the huge canine who at this moment might be passing himself off as a former Bishop of Rome. The Ghost of Pope John Paul I will have to deal with the situation immediately.

There are two methods for ghosts who get into serious trouble back on temporal earth to continue their mission. The first and most obvious way is to pass a message on to one of the quick who is in the process of changing status. The message should contain a well edited plea for assistance. If the Ghost of Pope John Paul I were on a battlefront, an intensive care ward, or Democratic National Headquarters following a Presidential election, he would have no problem communicating with his bosses using this method. This not being the case, the Ghost of Pope John Paul I has to fall back on method number two. Why the Ghost of Pope John Paul I remembers these emergency procedures, and very little else, is covered in the Astral Workers Collective Bargaining Agreement of 1936, page 15, paragraph 3.

Method number two is an artificial procedure attractive to the majority of astral workers, but, since replacement of ghostly credentials is a complicated bureaucratic procedure, not as simple as replacing travellers' checks while vacationing at a Holiday Inn somewhere east of Hawaii, method number two is invoked more frequently than not. The Ghost of Pope John Paul I knows that even if he succeeds in making contact with the home office, his travel plans may be delayed for four to six weeks barring the occurrence of any religious festivals, which are numerous in the polyreligious sentiment in place upstairs at the present time.

The Ghost of Pope John Paul I begins preparations. Contrary to popular belief, radio and television transmissions carry numerous sideband signals undetectable to ordinary consumers, who are more than happy when the magic boxes they venerate in every room of their homes work at all. Joe Landgrantcollege is ecstatic when his favorite rerun sitcoms appear on the screen and a few extra lines in the picture don't make the slightest difference to him.

Various governmental and commercial agencies use sidebands on both radio and television to transmit signals undecipherable to Joe Landgrantcollege and, if they only interfere with his reception in a faint way, who's to know the difference - other than those few maniacs who inanely consider mass communication to have a vague connection with art? And we know the value of those people in the conglomerate board rooms of our destinies.

The Ghost of Pope John Paul I is aware of how these sidebands may be utilized. It's not a pretty thought, but the Ghost of Pope John Paul I knows he's up against it.

Taking a quart bottle of club soda from the refrigerator, the Ghost of Pope John Paul I says goodbye to the house where he's been parole officer for Imelda Marcos until her recent escape. He heads out into the wilds of Beverly Hills, his eyes constantly scanning the skies for the tallest man-made object he can find. It is now time for him to make broadcast history. In a small way.

After an hour of trudging through godforsaken wilderness, down to the last few ounces of his two litre bottle of club soda,

across one of the many canyons, the Ghost of Pope John Paul I
spots the object of his exploration. It stands tall, uninhibited by the
Beverly Hills tract houses encircling it, broadcasting for the free
world to hear how you really can get a better deal on a used car if
you take the time to drive an extra two hours to get the hell out of
Los Angeles County and into the real burbs.

After another hour of navigating through scrub brush and
scaling the side of a small canyon, the Ghost of Pope John Paul I
finds himself at the base of a television transmitter. It's fortunate
for him that they still have these dinosaurs hanging around modern
cities. Soon the cable revolution will make such structures
obsolete, and if he ever loses his wallet again, the Ghost of Pope
John Paul I will have to hang around critical-care wards longer
then suits his sensitive stomach.

The Ghost of Pope John Paul I looks to the top of the tower
and realizes the climb will take some doing. But he doesn't weigh
much anymore, so it shouldn't be too hard. Taking the last slurp
from his club soda bottle, the Ghost of Pope John Paul I begins a
hand-over-hand ascent of the broadcast tower.

"Because it's there. That's why." These are the words the Ghost
of Pope John Paul I can't rid from his consciousness during the
ascent. "Because it's there. That's why" means absolutely nothing
to him, but the words have echoed in his head since he clasped the
first steel crossbar in his right hand and pulled himself onto the
tower.

"Because it's there." Undoubtedly, this is a vague reference to
the great mountaineer, Sir Edmund Hillary, but the "That's why"
part is meaningless to the Ghost of Pope John Paul I. It's the
puzzling part of the phrase. "Because it's there" makes sense to
him. You can't explain certain motivations within the human
animal but one can stare at an incredibly tall mountain and give its

mere existence as the excuse for spending months of one's life climbing its sides when if you merely wished to achieve the summit, this could be effected in many less time consuming ways. "That's why" is the problem.

"That's why" is one of those phrases which used to drive the Ghost of Pope John Paul I absolutely bananas when he was among the quick. It usually was preceded by an even more loathsome phrase, "Because I said so" which drove the future Ghost of Pope John Paul I to distraction. "Because I said so" combined with "That's why", was enough to make the cleric find the nearest bottle of unconsecrated sacramental wine and bring it down to the neighborhood liquor store, where he'd barter for a more palatable drink.

The Ghost of Pope John Paul I's problem with the phrase "Because I said so, that's why" might have much to do with his Catholic upbringing. But let's face it, everything in a Pope's life has something to do with his Catholic upbringing, so we can pretty much rule out his Catholic upbringing when it comes to the phrase "Because I said so, that's why" since, if it were merely his Catholic upbringing which drove the Ghost of Pope John Paul I bananas on this point, he'd be driven bananas by everything in his life since, as previously mentioned, everything in a Pope's life hinges on his Catholic upbringing.

No, there was more to the Ghost of Pope John Paul I's distaste of this phrase than his upbringing. It has everything to do with wanting to become Pope in the first place.

No one becomes a Pope without massive amounts of preparation. The College of Cardinals collectively chortles whenever it's mentioned how U.S.A.P.S.'ians complain when it takes two long years for politicians to campaign for the Presidency. Two years don't constitute a drop in the bucket of

Papal politics. A cardinal who tried to pull an end run and campaigned for a mere two years would be lucky if he got out of Vatican City still within the good graces of the old boys in the College. No, these Roman guys take somewhat longer then two years to prepare for elections.

In modern times the process has been streamlined. Sure. During this century rumors have floated around concerning how some Popes were elected whose families campaigned for a mere two generations. Most Vatican insiders scoff at radical theories such as these but like most myths, when they persist for as long as this one has, there is a grain of truth to it.

When among the quick, the Ghost of Pope John Paul I was trained for the job from day one. Not the original "Day One" but the Ghost of Pope John Paul I's original day one. Fortunately, even the Ghost of Pope John Paul I can't remember anything preceding his fourth birthday but, judging from family records he came across while still among the quick, the Ghost of Pope John Paul I's family were grooming him for the job three generations before his birth. Tradition and belief in long shots are necessities in multi-generational businesses.

Which did not make for what the educated populace would consider the most normal childhood for the future Ghost of Pope John Paul I. Reared by parents who knew him to be destined for the ultimate gig, he took well to his lessons and training. He'd mastered most of the more arcane Latin rituals by the age of four and by age six could recite the traditional Mass inside out while doing a handstand. For this feat alone he became quite the neighborhood attraction.

As he grew older, the future Ghost of Pope John Paul I began to probe deeply into his accumulated knowledge and often would ask his teachers the ultimate "W" word. "Why?" "Why do we say this? Why do we do that?" These were the same questions posed by many of his preteen peers and for a time the future Ghost of Pope John Paul I was well satisfied with his teachers' answers. After all, he was still less then ten years old and kids that age usually go along with just about anything.

But don't forget this is no ordinary kid running around asking dumb questions. This is the future Ghost of Pope John Paul I we're talking about and by the time he reached ten years of age the questions he was asking were a bit too advanced for your average grade school teacher. If you want to drive a grade school teacher crazy, put a ten-year-old kid who uses the Socratic method into their class. You'll get the idea.

Every new concept the future Ghost of Pope John Paul I came up against would unleash a hail of new and interesting questions from him.

The future Ghost of Pope John Paul I was never a dummy as a child and soon the scope and complexity of his inquiries drove many of his teachers into early retirement. Unfortunately, only the teachers who were slightly intelligent themselves were made to suffer the pains which caused them to opt for retirement or other professions. One must be aware to be aware of one's inadequacies and, as the future Ghost of Pope John Paul I brilliantly displayed his tutors' inadequacies, only the capable experienced discomfort.

All of which stranded the future Ghost of Pope John Paul I within an elementary quandary. As the pool of intellect surrounding him steadily decreased, those of his teachers least capable to handle an intellect such as his own were soon the only tutors available for the future Ghost of Pope John Paul I. It's a numbingly effective cycle.

As the future Ghost of Pope John Paul I grew older and somewhat wiser, he learned to stop asking questions. Since the answers being given by his entirely unaware masters were lacking intelligent thought, the future Ghost of Pope John Paul I felt forced to adopt this unfortunate tactic. In learning this lesson he came to detest a certain phrase which would haunt him for the rest of his life, and beyond. "Because I said so. That's why."

This final retort of the empowered yet inadequate drove the future Ghost of Pope John Paul I into a period of silence which many in his village assumed would be the end of their campaign for a local pope. The elders of the community began an alternate plan to place the future Ghost of Pope John Paul I in a major monastery where he would retain some chance of benefitting the village, no matter that such a reduction of scale would be gargantuan.

Because I said so. That's why.

As the Ghost of Pope John Paul I finishes his climb to the top of the broadcast tower, he tries to remember the reason for his ascent. For an astral worker, the Ghost of Pope John Paul I is entirely too out of shape and while he rests atop a maintenance ledge near the main antenna, his breathing comes in short, shallow pants. The Ghost of Pope John Paul I checks his racing pulse and convinces himself he isn't going to die again. As the Ghost of Pope John Paul I examines the community below, he remembers why he's doing what he's doing.

The Ghost of Pope John Paul I gets to his feet. Now for the tricky part. Electrical engineering and other related sciences were never the Ghost of Pope John Paul I's forte. Not that he's totally unaware of the subject, it simply wasn't an area of academics towards which he felt enthusiasm. The Ghost of Pope John Paul I was given the basic course after leaving the land of the quick and now he hopes the lessons learned after he supposedly was through learning lessons will be of more than limited value.

The reality of television ghosts has been around since before the device was invented. Radio interference is a fact of electronic life. The astral work force never used radio for any form of travel owing to the multiplicity of transmitters and the potential of getting irretrievably lost. Television, with far fewer transmitters, maintains a simplified road map. The possibility of being irretrievably lost remains but the potential for wrong turns is significantly decreased.

Television became the venue for astral transportation that we know it to be today in the early 1950's. Before the 50's there were too few television transmitters. Astral travellers were limited to journeys within a single broadcast range. Today, with many overlapping transmission areas, moving as far a distance as across country becomes as simple as boarding a connecting flight in Kansas City. The difference between the early days of sideband travel and now, is the difference between central city subway systems and intercontinental railroads.

The Ghost of Pope John Paul I itches as transmitted waves pass through his corpus. He has a general idea as to the direction he should travel but he'll eventually discover the exact route through trial and error. The reverse use of television screens give astral travellers the only directions available during transit.

As the Ghost of Pope John Paul I attunes himself to the frequency of the transmitter, he hopes this trip will be less a trial than his previous journeys via this medium. But then the Ghost of Pope John Paul I remembers he's never previously travelled in this manner and knows of it solely in theory. It's communal memories like this that keep the Ghost of Pope John Paul I awake at night.

Honing in on an appropriate frequency, the Ghost of Pope John Paul I prays one last time and launches himself into the great video land of Southern California. With any luck the Ghost of Pope John

Paul I's travel plan will take him along the northern route. He knows it's moderately longer but the Ghost of Pope John Paul I has always wanted to travel through this portion of the United States of America and Points South.

Sideband travel remains as one of the more misunderstood aspects of the finalized astral labor contract. After many years of debate, a joint union/management committee arrived at the none too satisfactory compromise under which the Ghost of Pope John Paul I now travels.

Originally, the major bone of contention was whether sideband travel time should be considered time on the road or entertainment time. For years management held the position that sideband travel should be considered time on the road even though viewing sideband in this manner constitutes a major increase in daily base pay for the traveller. Management's objective was to make sideband travel as expensive a budget item as possible. They basically said damn the expenses, we don't want the work force down there joyriding all over the place and having too much of a good time. We need to know where they are and what they're doing.

Labor's negotiators took a polarly different tack. Remember, labor strategy among the post quick doesn't consist of the same priorities found elsewhere. Whereas quick negotiators would immediately be seeking new employment if they ever suggested basic wage scales were less than secondary considerations in negotiations, post quick union reps have to put up with management's refusal to let the most fundamental concepts of accounting go by the board. Accounting is the sole management tool available to keep tabs on the work force. If the numbers add up, management knows what's going on. If no numbers exist, control is lost.

Back to sideband travel. After marathon meetings of the union/management committee, the topic of sideband travel, in the classic collective bargaining tradition, was decided to the satisfaction of neither side. Labor's demanded sideband be treated the same way as any other form of communication and management contended sideband is actually a means of transportation and its users should receive per diem and vacation time equal to a day for each part of a day occupied in transit. Both demands were ignored. Today sideband isn't mentioned in the contract. Astral workers can take advantage of its many benefits as they wish. Unfortunately, management has virtually ceased training sessions in the technique. Everything is pretty much catch as catch can.

One of the three major non-cable networks within the United States of America and Points South uses an eyeball for its corporate logo. The Ghost of Pope John Paul I muses on this fact as he stares through the television screen of a typical suburban family living in one of the many outskirts of Los Angles. From his angle in the corner of another suburban living room, the Ghost of Pope John Paul I peeks at mom in the kitchen microwaving something in a plastic bag which, as it melts, appears to the Ghost of Pope John Paul I to be taking the shape of nothing in particular. Sis hangs in a corner of the room on the telephone. Dad relaxes on the couch sucking down a beer, reading the sports section. The only one who notices the Ghost of Pope John Paul I's image on the screen is Junior who immediately spews out a stream of vulgarity the likes of which the Ghost of Pope John Paul I hasn't heard since immediately after his election when one of his fellow cardinals took the final results rather poorly.

"We gotta get cable, dad, sets acting weird again." These are the last words the Ghost of Pope John Paul I hears from this fine upstanding household as he changes direction and heads further west. The image of a fourteen year old boy charging him, remote control in hand, stays with the Ghost of Pope John Paul I as he surfs a new broadcast wave.

Another joy of sideband travel is the way you never know where you're going to land. The theory, as far as the Ghost of Pope John Paul I understands it, says if you're attempting to reach a transfer point, you concentrate on areas where the transmission signal is weakest. The idea being that, as a signal falters, there will be another station broadcasting close by to serve the other side of the fringe reception area. On occasion, astral travelers have emerged from their impulse form, reshaped themselves into something semi-human, and actually hoofed it to another transmitter to continue their journey. But such instances are the exception. As most frequently occurs, the Ghost of Pope John Paul I will eventually find another television transmission station receiving the signal he's on. The proximity of receiver and transmitter facilitates his jump from one station to the next. Some technicians claim to have witnessed St. Elmo's Fire at their broadcast stations but the Ghost of Pope John Paul I knows the true reasons for these sightings.

It appears to the Ghost of Pope John Paul I to be an ordinary television transmission facility. Scanning the room he observes monitors tuned to numerous stations. Many, he correctly assumes to be cable and, with their confined range, of no use to him. Two men sit at a console surrounded by more switches and gewgaws than the Ghost of Pope John Paul I would care to imagine in his worst nightmares. Why human beings need so much technology is something he never understood while among the quick and in his present state he sees even less need for keeping life at such a manageable distance. After the two technicians sitting at the console pass from their present state into the next will come the time when they miss the human contact these machines never gave them. Too many machines and not enough people. But by then it will be too late to do anything about it. Being under certain vows while quick comes to the Ghost of Pope John Paul I's mind.

It's been a long time since the Ghost of Pope John Paul I has had a chance to view so much of present day culture. As he views the dozen or so monitors, excluding his own, he notices not much has changed.

He views as four major network discuss revolutionary goings on in Eastern Europe but this doesn't surprise the Ghost of Pope John Paul I. It's a set play and he was in on it even before his election. Nice to see things going even more calmly than planned. Moves like these always involve elements of risk. The rest of the news is the same old same old. Moving his glance to another monitor he observes scenes from a rerun he watched decades ago. Didn't hold up but none of them ever do. What ever happens to the actors? They have a moment in the sun then they disappear forever. But some people probably say the same thing about him.

Time. There's never enough time to really sit down, relax and watch some tube. It's a problem the Ghost of Pope John Paul I thought he was done with when he changed over but now he never has time for anything. Time to move on.

Leaping from receiver to transmitter doesn't have as intense an effect on the Ghost of Pope John Paul I's metabolism as leaping from semi-solid state into pure electrical energy did. Perhaps the novelty of his first transmission transition is something he'll never feel as intensely again. The Ghost of Pope John Paul I feels the electric charges emanating from his screen and he uses complete concentration to focus on his new target.

The signal he selects emanates somewhere in northern Arizona. It's a pity since using this channel eliminates the northern route the Ghost of Pope John Paul I hoped to travel. The southern route takes him into an area prone to electric storms which he's heard may have deleterious effects upon astral travelers unfortunate enough to be caught in transit during a major blow. He'll take his chances, not enough time to find the northern link. He'd be backtracking. Nobody has time to waste.

The jump itself is anticlimactic. Now, occupying a screen on the opposite side of the control room, the Ghost of Pope John Paul I barely discerns the vapor trail. The two technicians notice nothing. It's his first transmitter to transmitter jump but he feels like a pro. Go east old Pope.

BIOLOGY LAB REPORT

****

*   Forsaking rudimentary forms of shelter, subject moved with female human to area indicated on map as grid J-47.

*   No sign of previous experiment detected by humans. Alpha transmission readings normal. Subject unaware of implant.

*   Continued close scrutiny advised at present time owing to presence not identified which appears to be influencing experiment. More readings to be taken as opportunity presents itself.

*   Human subject #1 reunited with human subject #2 and interactions to be noted in subsequent reports.

****

TOUGH DAY

The compact human entity experienced a tougher day than she cares to remember. The show was as good as could be expected given the multitudinous restrictions built into the format but the compact human entity knows something's missing and can't put her finger on it. When you spend an endless day seeking answers to questions you've yet to formulate, you end up one exhausted compact human entity by day's end.

There are problems with any guest appearing on any show but today's collection was a bit more idiosyncratic than usual. Kicking off with a cooking lesson from a perfectly paranoid author never helps. The compact human entity sympathizes with the man since he is obviously attempting to launch a new career, but why did he have to choose her show to demonstrate his inadequacies as a celebrity cook? The compact human entity assumes the other gab shows nixed his act and if it weren't for her show's lack of established ratings, he would never have been booked. But Imelda and the compact human entity made it through the segment without starting any new blood feuds, so the author's appearance can't be the only reason the compact human entity is feeling the way she is feeling.

There's the truck driver who claimed he isn't a truck driver but actually someone continually cruising the highways searching for his pet dog. Why Imelda's producer insists on booking madmen is beneath the compact human entity's comprehension but being new to the talk show circuit, she has to bow to inanely experienced professionals.

The driver is on the show because of bees. It's obvious from the moment he trips over the curtain on entering the stage he's no professional. Still the compact human entity thinks he's cute, in a rurally inbred type of way.

Imelda makes her usual exaggerated fuss over the new guest. Must have been an all league pillow fluffer in her prime.

"Yes, yes, yes, yes, yes. Yes, you tell compact human entity and Imelda about all who come into your big truck - those nasty bees. Yes, you tell compact human entity and Imelda about nasty bees all."

The compact human entity knows by his expression her guest's having the usual problem following Her Convolutedness's syntax.

"Why, Imelda, don't you think our audience would like to know a little bit about our guest before he starts telling his story. Don't you think so, folks?" And like the pro she's become during the last few weeks, the compact human entity coaxes her audience into spontaneous applause aided by one hundred and twenty state of the art digital applause signs strategically scattered about the studio. She hasn't been sitting at Imelda's knee taking mega-voluminous notes for nothing.

As the audience's enthusiasm subsides, the compact human entity catches a slight shift in her guest's behavior. He'd arrived as a lumbering hick overwhelmed to be on the same stage as the former First Lady of the Philippines and Surrounding Suburbs, but during the forced onslaught of applause, the compact human entity gleans an aspect of self-satisfaction suddenly streak across his visage. In this one instant, the compact human entity bleakly realizes what she has helped create. She's come across the same situation innumerable times over her short years. Some poll watcher is picked to fill the seat of a Congressperson who's been indicted, because there's only four months before the election and the party needs a body to fill the chair since they know they're going to lose the election anyway because the only person they can reasonably hope to elect has been indicted and forced to resign.

Now these poll watchers taste the power of the spotlight for the first time in their life and anyone paying attention can see how it affects the saps. Suddenly people who never paid attention to them before ask to shake their hand. A majority of the unwashed masses aren't aware the saps will only be in Congress for the few months it takes to fill out the term. They could care less.

The compact human entity wonders if it has anything to do with poor lighting. She wonders if spotlight spill might cause a euphoria in some people way out of proportion to the attention they actually receive. She knew it as a child and over the years has struggled to achieve her own place in the arc light. She sees what it's done to the poor truck driver and the compact human entity isn't amused.

When wandering within the world of reflected celebrity, nothing appears the way it actually is. The compact human entity observes it in the truck driver, she recognizes it in herself, and the prime example is her co-host. The three of them achieved some semblance of stardom through little effort of their own. They were selected by accident, birth and marriage. Maybe it's this way for everyone.

The truck driver hasn't done anything to achieve celebrity, as little as his is. He's been involved in an accident and the world will notice him for the briefest segment of time until the oddity of his situation erodes. The great audience drops him into the spotlight then quickly extinguishes the illumination forever. For the rest of his life he'll try to regain the spotlight but like most people, he'll fail dismally in his attempts. The compact human entity pities him the way she pities most of the guests who attempt calling attention to themselves through this mindless medium.

How many, the compact human entity wonders, how many people construct their own self-worth from the attention of complete strangers? She knows that if her co-host's audience was completely taken away, Imelda Marcos would shrink to nothing in a matter of days. But as long as there remains a single person kowtowing to her, the former First Lady of the Philippines and Surrounding Suburbs will remain unaffected by the various arrows and slings of not so outrageous fortune that thousands of people, justifiably, continue flinging at her. Remove her audience and she disappears like a fairy tale witch doused by a bucket of Perrier.

The compact human entity isn't exempt from similar emotions. How often, while attending public functions with her father, would she bask in his reflected glory. Adults sought her opinion on topics which didn't matter to her in the least. As she grew older, reporters questioned her on topics where her expertise was nonexistent and then broadcast her response on network television as if anything emanating from a mouth such as hers was newsworthy for no other reason than her being a blood relative of someone who once wielded an almost indefinable lack of power. The compact human entity is aware her opinions on various current affairs are meaningless but the media manipulates her in a way she never will entirely understand.

But it's not the same for instant celebrities. She watches the truck driver attempt a return to normalcy after his network cable debut on "Midday Albany". How can life ever be the same for him? He will spend the rest of his time sitting in the same cab high above the road, playing an endless tape loop through his mind of an audience of free lunched shills giving him a thunderous ovation before he's had a chance to open his mouth. The compact human entity relishes the fact she'll never be brought so low. She knows her connections are solid enough to insure an audience almost every time she deigns to open her mouth.

The compact human entity brushes her hair and attempts to remember everything that's happened to her since she left for Los Angeles. The affair with the young man who promised her everything but left her holding the bag. Her being so embarrassed she couldn't call any friends or relatives to help out. Her taking demeaning employment to work off the debt, at the same time living in semi-disguise hoping not to be recognized by any of the millions of people who took inordinate interest in her while she was growing up in Washington. Having to lie to various government agencies concerning her whereabouts when she called in for routine security checks. It's a puzzling life as she looks back on it but it seems to be working out. She dreamed of having a national television show and now she has one. Even if it's only cable.

HOUSEGUESTS AND FISH

Professor Radigan should know better. He should have known better from the start. If strangers call and want to drop by, you don't automatically have to be nice and let them come over. Sometimes they never want to leave.

University housing wasn't consistently bad, now that Radigan has the time to think back on it. Limited space has its advantages. Houseguests being the example foremost in mind. If a few thousand bees decided to drop in at Radigan's previous digs, after a couple of days they'd have gotten the hint that there really wasn't enough room for everybody and they would have left. With the spaciousness of his new house, the bees seem far too content and Professor Radigan is forced to confine personal activities to his bedroom and the part of the living room nearest the entertainment center. The bees need him to operate the television's remote control. His houseguests are in the process of transforming the rest of his house into some kind of hive which Radigan finds extremely hard to comprehend let alone describe to the one or two people who now and then phone trying to determine the reason why Professor Radigan isn't coming down to the lab and why he hasn't been seen outside his house for weeks.

What's a person to do? Radigan thought of calling in the gendarmes when the swarm first started constructing their cells on his walls but he couldn't bring himself to actually make the call. What harm could a beehive do him, especially since the bees seem so neighborly? If he ever gets the chance to write an article explaining this experience, he's sure to be published in any number of scientific journals and the chance of crossing over into the profitable mainstream consumer magazine market should be well within reach.

Unfortunately, the believability of Radigan's version of events might make his tale only marketable among those magazines sold at supermarket checkout lines. If only the bees hadn't made it extremely clear to him during their last phone call how he wasn't to communicate with anyone else concerning their presence. Unfortunately, the last time the bees bothered calling him was over two weeks ago and now Radigan is falling victim to cabin fever. And his store of canned goods is running out.

The first day of the bees' occupation ended when everyone found a comfortable place to sleep. Radigan managed to chase a good number of the swarm from his bedroom and he guessed word got around. Radigan's bedroom is now the only area of the house completely off limits to his guests.

The assorted members of Radigan's household have come to an accommodation about how things are to be done. Being early risers, the bees get most of their busy work out of the way before Radigan gets out of bed. In the early morning hours the household is a flurry of activity as bees scurry about, warming up against the cool of early morning. Penelope has never been an early morning bee herself but with the new spirit of coöperation omnipresent among her fellow hive members, she faces her daily chores with an attitude resembling cheerfulness.

Penelope had a bit of a rough time during her first few days in the new hive. Call it homesickness, call it nostalgia, call it whatever you like, Penelope missed the old ways and it takes some getting used to whenever a society starts reordering their lives.

In her former hive, Penelope began the day in a similar manner as most other worker bees. They'd wake up, struggle out of their cells, buzz about as they warmed up their bodies, and performed basic calisthenics, a couple of wing bends here, some soft landings on friends' heads, and in general did what most insects do when there isn't a cup of coffee handy.

After a while the group leader would emerge from an early morning meeting with the division head and the mini-swarm which Penelope would call her own for the day would take off in search of targets of opportunity among the blossoms. The mini-swarm would disperse into smaller gathering parties and following ten hours of tending their gardens, the mini-swarm would regroup and head back to the hive. Penelope and her buddies would take care of the evening chores, exchange whatever news was collected during the day concerning targets for the next morning, then, as bedtime approached, they'd find themselves chatting about the good old days and drift gently into sleep, remembering victories of seasons past. It wasn't a bad life, even if it was boringly routine most of the time.

This new team was something else entirely. Instead of issuing orders first thing every morning, the new team made themselves scarce. It wasn't that they dallied away their mornings in bed or anything so unindustrious, it was simply when the bees from the old hive, Penelope among them, would get up in the morning, they were used to hearing someone issue orders for the rest of the day.

The new team seemed not to care if a few hundred of their fellow bees were flying around this new hive without a clue as to what activities were available for the rest of the day. As far as Penelope was concerned, the new team's ideas were fundamentally impractical.

She wasn't complaining. Penelope has never felt as liberated in her life. She knew in the end the new order would prove a boon for her and the rest of her hive. It was the way things started out which were not to Penelope's taste. Penelope tends to be a practical worker bee.

As the days go by, Penelope begins accepting her new role. After the first few days when most of the swarm hung around the new hive all day awaiting orders, things began straightening out. Sure, there were still a few bees who thought they could watch television with the walking/talking mammal for an entire day, but even they were starting to show signs of discontent with lives of complete and utter sloth.

There was no particular method to the madness of Penelope's new existence. Even Penelope squandered a few days simply hanging around, getting used to the new hive. But when she saw how the others managed to go about their business and still enjoy the increased amount of free time available, Penelope began to pull her own weight.

And it is astounding how productive this new hive has become. Even though they still have a number of malingerers who haven't discovered the joy of fending for themselves, the new hive's productivity is up by over two hundred and thirty percent. Penelope isn't sure how they come up with this figure but she knows what she's seen and what she's seen isn't half bad. The malingerers are fed from the hive's surplus and there is more than enough to go around. More for each member of the new hive than they'd ever seen before.

Since they no longer support a hierarchy of bees who do nothing other than give orders, write memos, compose reports, cater to the queen and, in general, contribute nothing to the creation of the commonweal, each individual member of the new hive is faring far better than when they occupied their former hive.

For years Penelope and her fellow worker bees were indoctrinated with the belief that the world is an extremely complicated place in which to live and the only way for bees to survive is to follow the advice and orders of their superiors since their superiors are the only ones with adequate information and intellect to properly comprehend the world about them. Now the world hadn't become any less complicated but the members of the new hive are beginning to understand survival isn't so difficult either.

On some days the bees didn't gather as much as was necessary for the hive to survive over an extended period of time. So what. This sometimes occurred in the old hive. When there was a shortage, the queen and the studs would regally take provisions from their storeroom and dole them out for the rest of the hive and the rest of the hive was supposed to be grateful since the hierarchy watched over them and took care of their needs. Big deal. Even though the new hive has only been in operation a short time, they were already stockpiling provisions in case of emergency. Within a few weeks the new hive would have enough in reserve to outlast the longest shortage within collective memory. Things were going rather well.

Penelope feels good about herself for a change. She'd never felt too poorly previously, but with the new organization, she starts experiencing many things she'd been missing. After much time pondering the subject, Penelope decides she likes the new hive a hell of a lot better than the old one and this isn't even taking into account cable television.

Penelope still doesn't know what to think about the television problem. Here she is, adapting moderately well to a new environment, not to mention the rest of the changes, and the alien bees keep suggesting it would be swell if the bees from Penelope's old hive tried to get in at least three hours a day viewing walking/talking mammal television. The alien bees are constantly talking about how it will broaden all their horizons if they could appreciate how walking/talking mammals exist. This leads to a few spirited discussions.

"Brother Bees, we appreciate your efforts in attempting to bring us out of the old hive's isolation. We do, however, question the need for the majority of us sitting in front of the electronic box for hours a day in vain attempts to decipher what walking/talking mammals say to one another. Couldn't we put this time to more effective use by, say, gathering more provisions and stockpiling them in case we run into any of the natural disasters we know so well."

"A valid point, Sister Bee, it's one we've discussed often. We're more than willing to talk about it some more. You may be right on this one."

"But, Brother Bee, if you think I may be right on this point, why do you and your fellow travelling bees suggest we view so much of the walking/talking mammal's electronic box?"

Penelope always enjoys hearing these debates even if half the time she hasn't the slightest idea what brought the participants to this particular point of discussion.

"Sister Bee, in our present situation we have to face certain realities, no matter how painful they may be. We live in a world where for centuries upon centuries bees have conceded control to walking/talking mammals and other animals. We have been satisfied with the path of mere survival. We can survive practically any eventuality. Our brother and sister insects adapted themselves so well that even if the walking/talking mammals were to unleash their colossal heat machines and destroy everything they have built, themselves included, we insects would survive. But this reliance on survival has been accompanied by a price.

"Sister Bee, bring your collective memory back as far as it can go. You will recall a time when this world was truly a land of milk and honey. Long before walking/talking mammals began their construction phase, we bees created undefended hives which would dwarf walking/talking mammals' highest skyscrapers. But as walking/talking mammals took up tools, we retreated into social structures designed to guarantee our survival. Guaranteed to maintain our existence, but the cost was our freedom."

"But, Brother Bee, we never felt this lack of freedom. We were content where we were. Survival should be the paramount concern to the life of the hive. Take away survival and no bee will enjoy any benefit of existence."

"Quite true, Sister Bee. But there are many ways for us to realize this same objective. What was good for survival of the hive was good for survival of the hive. There can be no rational debate to the contrary. Never let it be said social custom should be discarded in a casual manner. When the need for a new defensive order presented itself eons ago, we organized ourselves into hives to assure survival. The existence of our new hive merely illustrates the fact that we have survived.

"We've survived well enough to do away with old fashioned defensive hives. We are now capable of creating a new hive, a hive where each and every bee can fulfill his or her destiny without the rigid restrictions once necessary for survival. I almost said "mere" survival. Survival is never "mere". The new hives present a testament to our survival. The new hives present a testament to our willingness to bring our creativity, our essence, into a greater theater. We have nothing to fear. We understand we can survive the most dire circumstances."

"Brother Bee, I believe most of us comprehend the need for change. But what does change have to do with viewing the walking/talking mammals' electronic box. We know it's a form of communication for them but we have our own ways and consider ourselves capable of conducting the proper affairs of the hive using standard methods."

"Distance, Sister Bee. Distance. Our dance and other communication techniques were created for solitary hives, existing great distances apart, who virtually never communicated with one another. We now know it's possible for hives to communicate over tremendous distances utilizing the walking/talking mammals' electronic machines. Tools such as these can be of great service to any hive. Weather forecasting being not the least of their benefits. We're not saying anyone should be forced to use the walking/talking mammals communication systems. What we are saying is hives should be aware of these tools and possess the knowledge to utilize them. Never lose the dance or chemical trails but add the knowledge of these electronic devices to the hive's collective memory. You never know when they might come in handy."

Penelope is beginning to follow the conversation. It puzzles her. But then again, almost everything that's happened lately has been puzzling.

"We understand your desire for the hive to have the ability to utilize these tools, but instead of our actually utilizing these electronic devices, you're suggesting we learn how to decipher the messages and by deciphering the messages we're learning a great deal about the habits of walking/talking mammals. I still don't fathom of what possible use this knowledge will be to us. Certainly you're not suggesting we interact with walking/talking mammals?"

Penelope is somewhat surprised with herself since she was the one who asked this last question. Penelope isn't used to this new Penelope. Another puzzlement.

"Interaction, Sister Bee, is already under study at some hives. What's more, we're experimenting with it right here. What else would you call taking over the hive of a walking/talking mammal and making it our own?"

"Understood, Brother Bee, but what have we to gain from learning the ways of walking/talking mammals? They are on a path to extinction themselves. We should concern ourselves more with the survival of the hive than with learning foreign ways."

"True, walking/talking mammals are on the way to eliminating themselves as viable life forms on this planet but this may be the reason we need to learn from them right now, before they eliminate themselves, and the knowledge they accumulated during their span. Knowledge of a poison does not necessitate our ingesting the same poison. We have to know what to avoid as well as what to do. You can learn much from a dying teacher."

Penelope enjoys this conversation more than she's enjoyed anything, other than the first time she managed navigating her body in three dimensions without crashing. Penelope realizes this is similar to learning how to fly. The exhilaration Penelope feels within this new hive is as liberating as the first day she managed to fly out of the hive into the great world she is now learning to appreciate.

The discussion between her old hive mates and the alien bees continues endlessly. They find no greater pleasure than describing the situation in which they presently find themselves. Then, almost miraculously, the description they create begins existing in the real world. Ideas and experiences Penelope never considered possible in the old days, if she'd been capable of imagining such outlandish events, are hers for the thinking.

CORPORATE STRESS RELIEF

Little Aloysius begins to see the light. There are not enough hours in the day to deal with the nonsense his supposed "star" dishes him. What the hell is talent? Talent is taking perfectly ordinary people, telling them what to say and how to act, throwing them in front of a television camera and letting the audience identify with the schmuck because the schmuck makes the same mistakes the audience wishes they could make. Once you get the audience identifying with the talent, the rest is gravy. Or the best canned you can find.

Little Aloysius has the old bag wrapped up in such an elegantly convoluted contract that not even fifty code breakers fresh out of NSA training school could unravel all the legalisms, not even on their best day. And she owes him. She owes Little Aloysius big. If it hadn't been for him, she'd still be dusting hallways for the real skinny guy. Little Aloysius discovered her and whatever she makes from then on is his. Not twenty percent, not forty percent, not eighty percent, one hundred percent of everything. He has her for the next seven years and he has her on simple salary. God, life is good.

Let the hag take her bows. Let her think she's running the show. Little Aloysius has the other one under contract as well. Unfortunately, she gets paid more salary but Little Aloysius doesn't have the same leverage he has with the "STAR". Little Aloysius has plans for her too, and with advances and personal loans, and given the show stays on the air a minimum of two years, Little Aloysius should own the other one, body and soul by the start of the third season.

It's a wonderful life. It's a wonderful country. Where else can a mangy mutt like himself come out of the backwoods and become one of the biggest movers and shakers on national cable television. And the government can't tax him at all. Even the IRS isn't about to make a federal case against a dog. Fools. Everything is written off as company mascot expenses. Taxes? Little Aloysius laughs.

Back to everyday reality, Little Aloysius has the aching feeling again. It might have something to do with the big kid but Little Aloysius doubts it. He gave the kid a shot. National exposure. What more could he do? And the kid blows it by showing overexposed snapshots of Little Aloysius and asking the audience to help find his dog. Give me a break, will ya? Where is it written a dog has to be faithful every day of his life? Little Aloysius feels a pang of remorse. When is the kid going to get with the program?

This is a problem Little Aloysius has dealt with since before he left the woods and began his real life, his true vocation. It began with feelings of stagnation in the woods. It escalated as he traversed the country. It exploded when he met the Marcos female and managed to convey them both to New York by speaking bad Italian and flashing his stolen ID. After he cut the preliminary deals, the conflicting emotions came on stronger. When will it stop? When will Little Aloysius again feel content? How can he overcome his desire for control and power? When is that idiot secretary going to bring him the Denver overnights?

Sometimes it's too much for a canine with Little Aloysius sensitivity and intellect. Little Aloysius weighs the question. He knows he's unique since every canine he encounters on the street while taking one of his secretaries out for a walk is an unabridged dunderhead. Where do these hounds come from? They can't be from this planet. How do they survive using one millionth of the brain power at their disposal. Why does Little Aloysius frequently consider himself to be a freak of nature? What interest rate will be available if next quarter's gross exceeds last quarter's gross by eleven percent?

Presumably, something singular must have happened to put him in such a unique position. Yeah, he'd won the damn lottery - that's what happened. He'd won the lottery and now Little Aloysius sits in his office and doubts his abilities.

-It's mine. Everything is mine. Nobody gave me anything. I earned it myself. When I saw the opportunity I took it. I did nothing illegal. Even the dragon lady admits as much. She signed the deal when I convinced her I could get her out. She wanted out, she took the deal. Nobody forced anything on her.

-But that's not the answer. It's like when I began to read. Boy, I missed so much being out in the woods without Forbes magazine around. The big kid didn't have a clue as to the goings on in the real world. Not a clue. Then, when I started reading the literature, everything made sense. There's cause. There's effect. As long as you distinguish one from the other and know when to act, you can't lose. You can't lose much. Nobody's on the money all the time.

-Remembering helps. Thinking about anything helps. It's the history of the past years, without the slightest attempt at conscious thought, which hurts. Decades of my damn life down the drain watching a big kid chase sticks. Life equity washed away by spring rains. But that's water under the corporate bridge and if you dwell on past miscalculations eventually life comes a cropper.

Little Aloysius lifts himself from the daybed and scampers across the room to the office he keeps for the secretary who smells best that week. It's tough these days to find help with an agreeable aroma.

She's using one of those acrid chemicals on her paws. Little Aloysius fights off the desire to leave her alone and go back to the daybed in his office which he keeps smelling the way rooms are meant to smell. She'll be replaced, but for the moment, Little Aloysius's desire to get into the outdoors overwhelms his impulse to give personnel a quick call so that this one will be standing on the unemployment line tomorrow morning.

-Keep it up, kid. You've got a real short future in this business.-

Which Little Aloysius's secretary, Fran, hears as a bark. Putting the bantam brush back into the bottle of nail polish, giving the cap a twist, Little Aloysius's secretary looks at her boss standing in the doorway. For her, Little Aloysius is the personification of the definitive working class nightmare. From out of nowhere comes the pet of a mega-celebrity to run one of the largest entertainment companies in the greater Albany area, leaving the locals the drudge work.

-How's it figure? How's it figure when so many people work so hard for so long, to have the position of their dreams expropriated by some cross between a collie and an obese St. Bernard? How's it figure?-

Little Aloysius clears his throat to get the fool's attention. One of these days he's going to employ a human who actually knows how to work. He knows it's a dream but canines need dreams to get through the day.

-How's it figure? Two years of business school and I'm stuck taking dictation from an executive with paws. It makes no sense. If it weren't for the money.-

Little Aloysius glances at the clock and clears his throat again. Finally, the secretary grabs her coat and the leash, and this relatively disproportionate combination makes its way to the elevator.

Outside.

Little Aloysius is free. He doesn't particularly mind the office but he doesn't care for it either. Outdoors is where a dog belongs. Outdoors where Little Aloysius can breath the air in gulps without worrying about the central air recirculation system, humidity control and whether or not a two degree drop in average temperature during the following quarter will or will not affect the ability of the firm to collateralize fifteen million dollars in post-junk bonds soon to hit the market and in which Little Aloysius has more than a passing interest. Outside where dogs run free.

Except for the leash. Except for the collar attached to his leash being held in the acrid smelling paws of the secretary he intends firing before today's end of business.

-Something's wrong here. I'm at the pinnacle of my career. I completely control and am majority owner of the hottest talk show on national cable television, yet I can have my chain pulled at any moment by a business school graduate who will be standing in the unemployment line this time tomorrow. Can't be right.-

Little Aloysius's secretary wishes she could find the right man to liberate her from this corporate nightmare. This isn't what she'd planned for a career. She remembers her word processing professor at business school saying the most important weapons in her arsenal were a few private macros (Shift-F9, Del-F2, Alt-F5 were some of her favorites) which she should keep to herself for her entire working career.

-But what's the point in knowing how to run an organization when the power constantly shifts from one lap dog to another? Nobody ever said a secretary's life was easy. I expect my fair share of life's knocks, but putting up with a continually drooling executive on a leash is too much.-

Little Aloysius could care less about his secretary's feelings even if he had the sensitivity to notice her enough to read her mind and divine her thoughts. He's in the street now and there isn't anything more invigorating for a fully mature male hound than catching the aroma of hundreds of bitches who have recently strolled the same path. Invigorating.

Dragging the secretary by her leash, Little Aloysius heads into the park.

-Off paved streets fast. They're murder on the paws. One thing has to be said about humans, they made the roads, then they made the shoes. It's the great marketing idea of all time. Let's construct countless hard paved roads so we can peddle the rubes shoes made from rubber and leather. Damn things will need new soles and heels every couple of months and shoemakers will make a killing. Shoes are almost as disposable as bottle caps. Use them for a short time then toss them away.-

Little Aloysius turns his head giving Fran the once over.

-Never could figure why humans enjoy being dragged around on a leash so much. Must give them a thrill to be physically attached to vital life forms now and then. They isolate themselves as much as possible from nature, and when they finally feel the need to go outside, they attach themselves to some poor canine so they won't get lost. Pitiful creatures. Really.-

A lone human strolls the chilly park this December afternoon, crackling twigs underfoot, ignoring all others. A smattering of snow cover remains from the seasonal storm which struck three days ago. Little Aloysius wants to run free but knows his insurance company won't cover any accident unless he drags along a human being. The insurance company doesn't care what human he drags along as long as it's an adult specimen. He'd break loose from the leash in a flash if he wouldn't jeopardize his entire company with such a foolish caprice. Little Aloysius wonders if he's adhering to human dictates too much.

-Simmer down, Sparky, take inventory.-

Little Aloysius catches a particularly feminine scent, launching him into momentary semi-romantic revelry.

-I'm working too hard. There has to be a bitch in this park with my name on her. The only thing I have to do is take my time and she'll find me. I know how to strut.-

Little Aloysius intones a pitiful howl, startling his secretary. Jerking his leash, Fran is confronted by Little Aloysius's menacing bare teeth inches away from her face.

-Chill, little lady. You don't know who you're dealing with here. Count the teeth. Count the big teeth. Count the teeth which have torn rabbits in two. Count the teeth that mutilate squirrels on a daily basis. Count the teeth which make the difference between survival and death. Count the teeth, and if you tug on this chain one more time, they will leave an indelible impression upon your very essence.-

This is transmitted to Little Aloysius' secretary via another low, threatening growl. Fran doesn't grasp the entire message but manages to sense the gist. She loosens her grip on the leash.

-Humans are far too inferior a species to maintain the dominant role on this planet. The two network jerks I dealt with yesterday wouldn't last as canines any longer then it took their stomachs to empty. Fools. Thought they could take advantage of a poor little doggie. Never considered international residual points in the contract's second and third year. And they think they've got it made.-

Continuing his prowl, Little Aloysius drags his poor underling through sections of the park infrequently visited by mammals of the upright two legged variety. He has to stop his prowl when low hanging branches and other obstructions impede the advance of his human insurance policy. It's slow going but Little Aloysius is on a trail he knows will pay off.

-There's a scent in the air. There's a reason I've done the backbreaking work I've done. Maybe she's around the next bush. Hurry up, honey, cut some slack on the leash.-

Little Aloysius puts his nose to the ground and pursues traces.

-Not long ago. Not too long ago, she was here. Which direction?-

Raising his head, Little Aloysius takes in the segment of park scannable from his height. Fran, three feet higher, spots a dog urinating against a tree thirty yards away. She gives the leash a tug in the opposite direction.

-This one is going to enjoy the unemployment line. She works on my memos for the entire day and never gives me lip, but take her out of the office, give her token authority like this damn leash and suddenly she imagines she possesses authority. I have to do something about the situation. Right now.-

Confronting his companion, Little Aloysius again flashes his pearly yellows. He pauses as the realization of imminent attack despondently dawns upon the face of his none too bright underling. Fran releases the leash as Little Aloysius lunges at her.

-Midlunge. Midlunge she finally gets the idea. Midlunge. Damn it's good to be on the attack again. No silly board room maneuvering. No country club viciousness. I'm talking serious blood lust here.

-When does she decide to get smart and give up the leash bit? Midlunge. Can't maintain proper enthusiasm. The killer instinct is gone. But I'm free. That's what it's all about.-

It isn't a particularly graceful midflight correction achieved by Little Aloysius, but it does save the soon to be unemployed Fran from what might amount to a serious bill from any reputable, discount, plastic surgeon.

He lands squarely on his feet and avoids twisting an ankle. Fran gawks at Little Aloysius with a mixture of surprise, shock, terror and relief. Little Aloysius tosses her a parting glance as he sprints away in the opposite direction of his secretary's original tug.

-They think you don't know what they're doing when they lead you away from something. I'm aware of what's going on in their little minds. Damn insurance company. Damn network. I know what I want.-

Little Aloysius does indeed know what he wants. He even sees what he wants. The bitch can't be more than twenty yards away as Little Aloysius closes in at near full velocity. The bitch turns her head sensing Little Aloysius's approach. A look of panic then acceptance. Little Aloysius salivates all over the park grass as he approaches the object of his salaciousness. The bitch begins trotting away. Impact occurs with Little Aloysius traveling twenty-five miles per hour and the bitch ambling along at a sedate ten.

Fran regains her composure. Not being aware of any established procedures to follow, she sets off in search of her boss. It wouldn't be proper if she came back from this noontime soirée and reported to the rest of the company that she'd lost the boss during a walk in the park. It definitely would reflect on her efficiency and she is certain few of her future secretarial assignments would be as prestigious as the one she's on now. She has to find the boss or it's the end of her national network cable career.

Little Aloysius tries remembering overnight ratings from the Canadian Maritimes. He tries remembering the names of the Brady brats. Anything to avoid focusing on the job at hand. For the thousandth time he wonders if he's becoming too human.

-Stay right where you are, honey. This isn't going to hurt a bit.-

Concerned he may become locked into a position where his supreme negotiating abilities would be of limited use, Little Aloysius rests his chest upon the bitch's back, replaying through his mind the various options available when he becomes programmer for the network.

It's not like Little Aloysius would ever consider taking such a mundane job as head of programming, it's just that whenever he feels a loss of motivation, he always comes up with another job he could take which might prove more interesting than the one he's engaged in at the moment. Not that the job he's completing at the moment isn't engaging enough.

The bitch squirms under Little Aloysius's weight.

-Corporate structures must be made to conform with the specific canine needs of myself and those who will follow. Steady there, bitch, this is only going to take a little longer. Responsibilities for specific decisions have to lie with the individuals making them. Obfuscation of lines of authority will necessarily be replaced with a sharper focus on individuals. This will, for the short term, leave the corporation at greater risk, but the elimination of redundancy and the potential for creative thinking far outstrip the quarterly based mentality which creates the vast word processed memo flow engulfing corporate U.S.A.P.S. today.-

Fran arrives on the scene during a moment which would be exceedingly embarrassing for her if her boss were of the usual three-piece suit variety. She is appalled. She is flustered. She is perplexed. She wonders if there is any way to get a promotion out of this? What does the employees' handbook have to say concerning intraspecies dating? Fran realizes there is no career advantage to be garnered by observing two loose mongrels go at it. She retreats.

Little Aloysius can't remember when he's had a better time than right now. Even with the eternal corporate politics he feels obligated to review at this point, he finds himself having more fun than he's had in months. Not since before he left the woods and the big kid. Not since before he went chasing after what he assumed was another one of those people who only came to the woods in the summer. Not since he became fascinated with the pulsating lights in the sky. Not since before they used the light to hurt his head. Not since he began remembering everything he's ever known. Not since before he began to become human in uncountable ways. Not since before.....

-What am I doing here? I hardly know this bitch. She could have been anywhere. Who knows what diseases she might be carrying around with her? I should have brought along some protection. What if she has a litter? The bitch could sue me. How will it look in the trades? `NAT CAB NET EXEC LITTERS TOWN WITH UNKNOWN BITCH'. We're producing a family oriented talk show. How can I oversee a public offering of stock if I have a paternity suit hanging over my head? Damn, I wish this bitch would hold still.-

Little Aloysius teeters between two worlds. He knows if he continues along the course he started this afternoon, his entire career could be in jeopardy. His present project, taking a washed up hag of a former dictatress out of the hands of a post-quick parole officer and launching her into the wide world of popular gab/talk/philosophy/commercial tie-ins, would be blown. This really could do a number on his Nielsen's.

-But it feels so good.-

Fran has seen enough. Not only does she have to suffer the humiliation of being the only secretary in the organization deemed subservient enough to rate a subspecies boss, now she has to hang out in a public park while the boss puts it to the first stray bitch he finds. Something has to be done about this.

Little Aloysius can't get his mind and body to coordinate properly. This is not the time to think about anything other than the work at hand. Or paw, if you demand accuracy. He tries a few Oriental focusing exercises the folks down in personnel relations have been shoveling around the corporation in lieu of raises, and for a short time the overwhelming sensuality of the event does drive thoughts of the office from his consciousness. But it doesn't last long enough. The bitch seems bored.

-I don't even know her name. What would the guys back in the kennel say about this? Sure, they'd be all for it. As long as I told them the story with acceptable graphic detail. Why not? `As I approached, I could see by the dewy fur on her hindquarters she would willingly engage in an afternoon's entertainment.' Great. I'm already aroused, I don't have to start telling stories to help it along. Maybe if I found an inexpensive, independent producer (redundant), we could whip up an eight or ten week series on the great bitches of history. An adult "Wild Kingdom". Could work.

In the morning have the acrid secretary fax out a memo before I sack her.-

Which would have been a wonderful idea if Fran hadn't come to a few conclusions of her own and decided to act even without using the LAN network the company recently installed to make sure no single individual could ever be blamed, or take credit, for anything. This would be an independent action on Fran's part. The company would disavow all knowledge of her actions. This action would be completed entirely on her own. A concept totally alien to corporate culture. Fran feels right about it. She can relate.

As Fran approaches Little Aloysius and the new love of his life, she removes a newspaper from her purse and scans the headlines. She'd carried the paper along in case her boss, in the everyday way dogs do in parks, was indiscreet. Seeing nothing worth reading on the front page, Fran rolls the paper tight. She advances on the courting couple.

-Too much. Too much to take even for an old canine like myself. Let's see if I've got this straight. As I become more like the humans, I become less and less like others of my species. This makes sense since how can I remain similar to my own kind as I become more human and the other hounds remain the same.

-Now, since there's no way for me to live totally as a human being, there must be some accommodation to my houndness. This walk in the park being a prime example of said accommodation.

-Fine, so far. It's nice, when for a change, I'm capable of following my own train of thought. Steady, honey, only a little longer.

-Does it really come down to a matter of having to decide which of my natures to follow? I'm a canine. This is a certainty. Every time I look in the mirror, there's no denying I'm not like the mammals I work with every day.

-I don't think like other dogs. There has to be a simple explanation for this anomaly. Whereas every dog I've met since leaving the woods has been incapable of communicating with me except on the most base level, I know what they've been saying and it bores me to tears. I need the companionship of fellow hounds, but having to listen to their jabbering about scents, food, mates, trees, and assorted nonsense, doesn't endear them to me at all.

-Somehow I'm an inhabitant of both the canine and humane worlds. Certainly didn't ask for it. Wasn't in any master plan I created. How can I maintain a stable existence when my mind exists on two non-intersecting planes? The two worlds coexist but have nothing in common with one another.-

As Little Aloysius continues his dual pursuits of reproduction and reduction, Fran pauses to read a newspaper article which catches her eye. Unrolling the paper she learns a swarm of "killer" bees is approaching the Albany area. According to the reporter, an enormous swarm recently bypassed Buffalo and appears heading in the general direction of this great capital of New York (Mostly The City and other Places with Trees) State. The piece recounts how motorists rubbernecking the passing swarm contributed to major traffic foul-ups responsible for at least one death. An eighty-four year old gentleman's life support system failed when the technician responsible for the machine's repair was held up in the bee prompted traffic jam. "Killer" bees on the prowl.

The article ignites a few embers within Fran's underutilized consciousness. She vaguely recalls one of the first guests to appear on "Midday Albany". Wasn't he a truck driver with an odd story to tell about being attacked by a swarm of bees primarily interested in using his fax machine?

This could be Fran's big break. What does a producer do other than come up with stupid ideas for shows designed to seduce the audience, then fail to deliver any of the promised entertainment, while at the same time luring the viewers into switching on the show just one more time.

This could be the one. Fran sees it on a mental 19-inch Sony Colortrack screen before her very eyes: a live remote broadcast with Her Swellness and the compact human entity leading the truck driver in a discussion of the menacing approaching swarm. Fran sees herself enthroned in the control booth calling the shots.

Little Aloysius arrives at a conclusion. The conclusion isn't the one he'd imagined he'd be making at such a delicate time but it's none the less a conclusion he should have concluded he'd make ever since leaving the woods where he'd spent most of his time watching the big kid enjoy himself immensely throwing sticks which Little Aloysius would bring to him whenever Little Aloysius thought it would be fun to watch the big kid throw sticks.

-You can put up with what life deals you to a certain limit. I had nothing to do with becoming the mental genius I've become and I wouldn't have put myself in the position of being the only humanely conscious canine in existence if the deal had been up to me. But it wasn't. I have to confront life with the hand I've been dealt.

-Stay still, honey, you might enjoy this sooner or later.

-It's time. It's time I stopped kidding myself. I can't adapt to the humane world. There's no pleasure there. Boy, this bitch has great fur. It's time I went back to the woods where I can roam around on my own, and if I want human companionship, I can look up the big kid and see if he wants to throw some sticks. I got a kick out of it. This office life is too confining. Some humans find it too confining too. Maybe I'm becoming a different kind of humanized canine.

-This could make a sort of sense. Let's suppose for a thousand years, let's say ten thousand years, every canine has had this special type of brain within themselves, but for any number of reasons they have denied its existence. Let's say my ancestors knew they were superior to humans in every conceivable way, but they let humans take the upper hand due to preservation instincts or something equally mundane. Let's say I'm not the first canine cursed with superior intellect but I am the first to realize its potential and act on it, probably in thousands of years. Perhaps I'm not alone in this world of innocent caged canines and liberated criminal humans. Perhaps if I communicated to others of my species we could do something to correct this abominable situation. I could start now.-

-Yes, you could.-

-Damn straight I could.-

-You could start by paying more attention to what you're doing at the moment.-

-I always pay attention to what I'm doing.-

-Well if you paid more attention to what you're doing maybe I wouldn't have you on my back and we could commence a civilized conversation.-

Which is when Little Aloysius explodes. And being the type of dog he is, Little Aloysius explodes in more ways than one. He explodes with the dogness he's been exploring for the past fifteen minutes which, in and of itself, sets a record for inter-canine relations. He explodes with joy, realizing he has made contact with an equal of his own species. Little Aloysius doesn't understand how the contact came about, how this one bitch, of the many thousands he's contacted is the only one who made contact with him other than to clarify whose tree is whose. He explodes with wonder realizing this could be the commencement of a second coming for the entire canine species. He explodes physically as he realizes his own secretary has whopped him on the side of the head and he's plummeting to the ground, already detached from the true love of his life. He doesn't know her name.

Fran hovers over the spasmodic body of her newly deposed boss. The coup d'état is a success. As she watches her boss writhe on the ground, a warm, liquid tranquillity encompasses her being. It's the calm after an adrenaline rush. The top dog is dead. Long live the top dog.

Little Aloysius feels funny. He doesn't feel funny like he used to feel funny whenever a human took it into their mind to whop a dog on the side of the head with a newspaper and Little Aloysius happened to be the closest victim they could whack. Little Aloysius knows his situation to be somewhat more serious.

The unknown bitch stares at him. His acrid smelling secretary looms above him like the ghost of a gathering thunderstorm. His vision dims. The bitch licks his face but Little Aloysius no longer comprehends her bark. Fran leans down and whops him on the other side of the head. This can't go on.

He can't think. Struggling to maintain consciousness, Little Aloysius tries remembering overnights from..... from somewhere. Somewhere there are trees. He struggles against losing it all.

-Somewhere there are trees, and bunnies to be chased. Overnights from Denver. Denver, the mile high city with demographics to make you weep. And trees. The most beautiful trees in the country. In Denver.-

The bitch lunges at Fran. Little Aloysius wants to tell his loving bitch it's all right. He wants to tell her not to bother. Let the humans be. They're more than content killing themselves. Fran steps back, avoiding the bitches teeth and with a backhand honed to lethal effectiveness during countless lunch hours at the midtown indoor courts, Fran manages to whop the bitch on the side of the head with her rolled up newspaper. The secretary's paper is doing its work far too well to be composed of mere paper. The bitch goes down.

Little Aloysius crawls the few feet to the bitch. She doesn't move. He looks to his former secretary.

-Another step on the corporate ladder?-

Fran moves to strike Little Aloysius in response to his growl but Little Aloysius disregards her threat and turns to the one dog he will forever truly love.

-If I'd known. If I'd seen through my petty desires. I've wasted too much time. Come so far. Come so close.-

Little Aloysius knows he's nearing the final precipice. Nudging the bitch's side with his snout, her body remains inert.

-Howl for the rest. How do I separate my howl from my being? Where's the sense in it? I am what I do. There is no separation. I die with my boots on. Unfortunately, it's a collar rather than boots. I'm leashed to my murderer. There will be no justice for this crime. There will be no satisfaction. Certainly there will be no retribution for my beloved. Humans will cart her away to the dump with the rest of the park's trash. And for this I've travelled the world. I've accomplished nothing.-

Fran watches as her boss expires at her feet. First she pokes the bitch with the newspaper, then she pokes Little Aloysius. After such a serious workout the now shredded newspaper reveals itself to be wrapped around a ball peen hammer. Fran, always aspiring to be the efficient secretary, carries the hammer in her purse at all times. To ward off muggers. To repair office equipment. Fortunately for her career, she's improvised another application.

With no reaction forthcoming, Fran stoops down and removes Little Aloysius's collar. Her plan is to have Little Aloysius disappear much as he appeared, from nowhere to nowhere. Let it remain the great unsolved mystery of national cable television. Already the concept of an unsolved mystery mini-series involving the career and disappearance of her former boss projects onto the Sony of her unconscious mind.

Little Aloysius feels the final restraint being removed from his body. He knows it's time to go. Attempting to nestle his body closer to his beloved's, he is aware he no longer has control over his corporeal being. His eyes remain open as he stares at the lush fur of his beloved's back. It's time to go.

-All I ever wanted was a network of my own.-

Fran gloats over her victories for a final instant then turns her back on the two lovers. As she heads back towards the office, she prepares the story she will doggedly maintain throughout the foreseen investigation and mini-series. She wraps her coat tight against her body and begins a mental shopping list. There will be money in this.

Little Aloysius's mind roams far afield. His eyelids close.

I'M A SURGEON,
NOT A STURGEON

Batbat   Never should have let you do it.

Vram   How was I supposed to know it would end up this way?

Batbat   All I had to do was stick with the manual and keep you out of trouble. But you insisted we use our initiative. Fine bunch of initiative this turned out to be.

Vram   Great. Blame it on me. Give me a hand with these.

Batbat   Never should have gone along with you. Unauthorized experimentation on indigenous populations. You know the rules.

Vram   I can fix it if you help me.

Batbat   You can fix it. Sure, you can fix anything. You can't even get us out of here and you're telling me you can fix this. You've never come across a problem like this before and you're telling me you can fix it. Bosh!

Vram   Well, I can.

Batbat   No, you can't. I'm telling you I'm not going to lift one solitary gram of flaccid muscle to help you. You hear me? Not a single gram!

Vram   If that's how you feel about it, I'll do it all by myself. They'll love it when they read in the journal that I accomplished everything myself. O.K., I was willing to give you most of the credit but now I'll have to confront every centimeter of glory on my own. I hope you know how you're condemning me to a future of undesired fame and fortune. You know I'm not the type who'll enjoy that kind of thing.

Batbat   I'm not buying any of this. Not for a second.

Vram   I understand how you feel. Imagine the todo that'll occur when they realize I've experimented with indigenous life forms and managed to pull off the big one. I won't be left alone for decades. They'll have me going to dinners and testimonials, and I'll tell them how I offered my partner the chance to assist, but he turned me down because he insisted on going by the book and I was the one who realized desperate times call for similar measures. You know how it'll make me feel? You have any idea how lousy it's going to make me feel having to tell them you totally dropped the ball?

Batbat   All I'm saying is you've already messed up. I don't believe messing things up some more will help us out.

Vram   You don't think I can do it?

Batbat   It's not a question of whether I believe you can do it, or whether I don't believe you can do it. We're not even supposed to be here. Can't you remember what our assignment is supposed to be? It gets to me sometimes too. Sometimes, I can't even remember what we're supposed to be doing. The only thing I know is we, definitely, should not be doing any kind of experimentation on indigenous populations. It's right here in the handbook. All you have to do is read it for once in your life.

Vram   You're right. It's foolish of me to insist. I mean, after all, we have so many tasks to accomplish. We can't fix this damn machine. We're stuck here. We have two members of an indigenous population with us and we're not going to do a thing to help them. I mean that's why we're here, isn't it? We're here so we can do absolutely nothing other than hang around and complain about how we can't fix this damn machine while members of the indigenous population cease to exist. I am reading you correctly, aren't I?

Batbat   You're making too much out of all this. Of course I'm concerned about the indigenous population. We wouldn't be doing what we're doing if there weren't a concern for each and every indigenous population. But we travel under certain restrictions. We are not completely free agents. I sympathize with your willingness to help the two of them; but we have to draw the line somewhere. Hell, we don't even have to draw the line, it's been drawn for us. It's simple, you have to consult the manual. We can't do it. Final word on the subject.

Vram   Can't say anything after that. Well, you're not going to try to physically stop me if I decide to go ahead with this, are you?

Batbat   I don't know.

Vram   Don't know? Certainly doesn't help a lot. Listen, I've got a deal for you. You keep doing what you're doing, trying to get us back on course, and I'll keep doing what I'm doing. Sound good to you?

Batbat   Sounds like I never even heard about any indigenous personnel.

Vram   Sounds good to me too.

ASSIGNED RISK POOL

Radigan wishes he were somewhere else. He wishes he were somebody else. He wishes he hadn't gotten up this morning. He wishes he hadn't gone to sleep last night. Most of all he wishes he weren't doing exactly what he is doing at this moment. He doesn't wish he was dead. But the thought does cross his mind.

He'd never done anything evil enough to deserve this. Radigan remembers most of his truly rotten acts and none of them, not all of them combined, total up to the type of heinous activity which deserves this type of punishment. Radigan knows he can't be totally objective on the subject, but giving himself absolutely no benefit of the doubt, his history of antisocial activity simply doesn't deserve this type of treatment. Some of his colleagues, yes; Radigan, no.

Attila the Bee. Is the bee army capable of a midwinter crossing of the Alps? Will the forces of civilization stop them on the banks of the Hudson? Will humanity be forced to kowtow to the King of the Bees? Tune in next week for the thrilling, concluding episode of "Radigan; Last of the Bee Kings". What else could he possibly think? This is the situation.

Looking to either his right or left, the only things Radigan sees, aside from the occasional piece of architecture and one or two skyscraping trees, are bees. When he manages to turn his head completely around, nothing can be seen other than the immense swarm. Far ahead he barely discerns the vanguard of this insect army. Radigan has never before felt so completely isolated.

Radigan's given up trying to figure out what the hive constructed for his transport. As far as he can tell, it's a cross between an Oriental emperor's throne and petrified cat's puke. As his one of a kind sedan chair is carried by who knows how many of the swarm, the one thing Radigan can do is relax and enjoy the view.

It's an odd story. As the bees settled into Radigan's home, the daytime's main social event became the viewing of an inane afternoon cable talk show. Radigan didn't understand the fascination the show held for the swarm and after a few days of hearing an aging tyrant do her best to destroy countless American pop standards, Radigan scheduled his afternoon nap for the hour during which the show polluted the airwaves, or cablewaves, whichever term *The New York Times* deems more appropriate.

Professor Radigan doesn't exactly remember how many weeks the occupation lasted. He remembers being in his house for a long time while the bees organized varied activities, and he stagnated. He knew what was happening. The bees exhibited behaviors far too similar to those he performed as a preteen when he was given an ant farm as an educational toy. For hours at a time Radigan would stare at the occupants of the farm, observing their organization and at times noting the personality of individual ants. Unfortunately, the situation was far too perfectly reversed, with thousands of bees observing a single human being. Radigan hopes he's a credit to his species.

And so it went. After an indefinite period of time, Radigan lost complete conception of time. As bees construction gradually enshrouded his home, Radigan became unable to distinguish day from night in any other way than through television programs. He could distinguish weekends from weekdays but this was due mainly to the absence of "Midday Albany" on Saturdays and Sundays and the preponderance of cartoons and sporting events. Somehow the bees managed to keep his refrigerator well stocked. There was a uniquely engineered ventilation system which maintained a constant temperature within the hive, Radigan's home, so Radigan's life was not a constant trial. With the continual hum of his home, Radigan soon realized he was being maintained by a life support system previously unknown on this planet. He slept, he ate, he was observed. Life was good.

This dreamlike state had to end and for Radigan the end came too soon. Somewhere in the recesses of the feeble excuse he once called his mind, Radigan realized the bees were up to something out of the ordinary. Ordinary for the hive which Radigan's home had become. One recent afternoon Radigan slipped out of his bedroom during "Midday Albany" and to his amazement discovered barely a third of the number of bees who usually could be counted on to gather in front of the tube for the show gathered in front of the tube for the show. And Radigan sensed the third who watched the show were uneasy being there. It was as if the bees wished they were somewhere else, where the real action was going on, but they were being forced to stay home while everyone else was out having a good time.

Radigan felt anticipation exude from each individual bee. Over the weeks he's been held prisoner within his own home (his telephone was now being answered by a most unique voice mail system), Radigan became sensitive to the emotional states of his house guests. He could never be sure he read their moods correctly but somehow Radigan is sure he could approximate the emotional state of individual members of the swarm.

He retreats to his bedroom to work on the problem. For some unknown reason the majority of the swarm has decided there are more important tasks to perform than the daily viewing of "Midday Albany". Obviously, this is a certain indication of intellectual maturation by the swarm. Perhaps Radigan will now be able to conduct a civilized telephone conversation with the swarm's mouthpiece rather than merely taking orders over the phone whenever the swarm decides the volume is too loud, or wants to scan the channels for a while to see if a more exciting show is on another channel. For a while there, Radigan considered forming a union of disenfranchised remote control operators, but on reflection realized there wasn't a large enough talent pool from which to draw membership.

For three days the swarm maintains this altered pattern, leaving Radigan to his own devices to try to understand why the change in behavior. The bees have loosened up considerably. Although they previously seemed content viewing the tube, Radigan noticed an increasing amount of what, for lack of a better term, Radigan termed "hive fever". But this incipient disease was now gone and although the swarm continued a daily watch of "Midday Albany" Radigan sensed anticipation in the community. Something was definitely up.

They came for Radigan in the night. Half in a dream Radigan imagines the door to his bedroom swinging open and thousands of his houseguests encircling him in his bed. With gentle persuasion they convince their host to emerge from his berth, leave the warmth of his room, and follow them to the front lawn.

The fairies are dancing. By the light of the scintillating moon, Radigan sees the swarm in its full glory. As far as he can see, which isn't very far since his view is obstructed by the very object he views, are the bees. Never, in what he now considers his rather limited imagination, has Radigan conceived of the overwhelming number of his houseguests. They absolutely occupy three dimensional space for blocks around. Radigan can only see as far as the end of his particular block but he knows for a certainty there is more to this swarm than his unassisted eyes can perceive.

In the moonlight Radigan sees the gargantuan swarm for the juggernaut it is, but he sees individual bees as well. Some of the swarm's members Radigan has come to know as intimates. He nods in recognition. He feels himself gently nudged to his left. Turning his body, he watches as the moonlight slowly illuminates a golden amber throne.

Penelope is excited. Penelope has been excited for the past two weeks. Penelope is having the best time of her life. Never before has she been part of such a massive project. And in this project she doesn't feel like a lowly worker bee at all. She hasn't felt like a completely insignificant member of the hive since she left her former home and with this project she knows her contributions to be of integral merit.

It was possible the alien bees knew how to construct the throne for the new "King Bee", but Penelope is the one who designed it and supervised construction. The alien bees knew they needed a way to transport the new "King Bee" but left it to the former inhabitants of the old hive to come up with a plan. In consultation with her peers, Penelope created the design and somehow was cajoled into organizing and implementing the project. She'd never before thought herself capable of such an undertaking.

The throne. A joy of beauty. Even Penelope admits it's wonderful and by nature she's more inclined to dismiss its existence as being as commonplace as a tree or a rock. But there is no denying it exists. An idea which once was a mere fly speck in Penelope's mind now exists in three dimensional space. It's entirely Penelope's. She's the first to admit she benefitted from massive help. Bees she'd never met previously spent days working side by side with her. Fellow bees she'd lived within inches of for her entire life but never known their names were now her friends. They created the throne together. But it was Penelope's idea.

She can't help it. She doesn't feel badly taking special pride in her work. Penelope knows she never would have been able to achieve this greatness without her companions but she feels accomplishment within herself. Sure, Harry, the drone, was the one who created the glue capable of holding together such an immense amount of weight. Sure, Sheila was the one who came up with the idea of the bees working in separate teams in order to make the project more manageable. Sure, Rhona was the one who had the engineering skills to create the structural drawings. But it was Penelope who had the original concept and it was Penelope who brought the disparate parts together. Penelope is proud of herself.

And now is when Penelope really starts worrying. What if her concept won't fly? What if when they take the new "King Bee" to his throne, and let him rest his royal buns in the seat, the entire throne collapses under the inordinate weight of a walking/talking mammal? What if when they attempt to maneuver the throne from its spot of glory on the front lawn it won't be budged? What if the walking/talking mammal won't sit in it at all? What if the patch Harry created as a temporary fix for a design flaw in one of Rhona's drawings fails? This is becoming too much for Penelope to take. And her friends are all looking at her as the walking/talking mammal is escorted to the throne.

Penelope wishes she'd never left her original hive. No, that's not what she feels but it's close enough. She wishes she were anywhere other than where she is right now, excluding the hive of her previous life.

-Can't take the pressure. Can't take the pressure. Who could take this pressure? They're all looking at me. Hey, guys, this isn't my fault. We worked on this together, remember? Any of you could have had my job. Remember when we were halfway through construction and none of you thought I had it in me to complete this damn thing? Remember how you kept after me to stick with it? Remember how you badgered me for hours on end not to give up on "our" project, and how you needed me to see the entire team through? Sure, you don't remember. The only thing you remember now is how I'm the one who said no to some of your harebrained ideas which would have lead to complete disaster.

-Wasn't it you, Rhona, who had the brilliant idea of reprogramming our cell structure in order to emulate the spinning capabilities of some spider I've never heard of in order to achieve the tensile strength you thought necessary. Give me a break!

-Now you think I may fail. Well that's always been one of the options. But I'm not going to fail. The hours of backbreaking work we put into this project is not going to be for nothing. One walking/talking mammal isn't going to ruin it for this gang. We're a team. We've worked as a unit our entire lives for the benefit of others but this one is for us. Nobody can take it away from us. We're going to win! The walking/talking mammal will sit on the throne and it won't collapse. You've got to believe! That's all.-

Which Penelope thought should be enough of a pep talk for any bee alive. Didn't actually reveal what she was thinking, of course, but she felt it part of her job. Part of her job which wouldn't be finished until the walking/talking mammal and the swarm arrived at their destination mostly in one piece. It really wasn't what Penelope was thinking at all.

Penelope wants to be anywhere else than where she is at the moment. She'd gladly spend the rest of her days sitting in front of the walking/talking mammal's electronic box not able to understand any of the signals being beamed at her, alone in the world where the only company she has is herself and an electronic box. Anywhere but where she is. She'd rather be freezing to death somewhere where it never gets warm enough to be able to fly. She'd rather be on the surface of the sun for the few seconds she'd be able to exist in such a hostile environment. Anywhere but here. Anytime but now.

She'd seen a throne on the walking/talking mammal's electronic box which she used as a model to construct the group's throne. The swarm was sitting through another long evening trying to absorb as much walking/talking mammal culture as possible. Penelope can't remember what the documentary they were watching was about, but she remembers being fascinated by the neat seat the subject of the documentary perched upon whenever his people came to see him. Penelope remembers the show had a tragic ending but the ending was one of the few items in the show she remembers. So much for originality in the arts.

And now the walking/talking mammal is only seconds away from road testing Penelope's creation. Penelope makes a move to escape to the inside of the house.

-I need a sip of water.-

Her group won't buy it. They buzz tightly about her, restricting her flight path to mere inches in diameter. She's blocked in. Penelope feels the panic streak through her vein.

-This isn't happening to me. I'm too young to be responsible for the success or failure of the swarm's master plan. What's going to happen when the walking/talking mammal, the new "King Bee", sits on the throne and it collapses? My own swarm will turn on me. They won't let me live. They aren't going to care about the budgetary constraints I was under. They aren't going to care the only bees I had to work for me were total neophytes to the business of throne construction. The only thing they'll want to do is find the bee responsible for ruining their plan. They'll want to know who insulted the "King Bee" in such a manner. They'll be screaming for blood.-

Penelope finally accepts her fate. She knows she can't run. She knows she can't fly. She watches as the walking/talking mammal, "King Bee", begins to take his place upon the throne. Penelope feels every ounce of energy within her bee body surge towards her brain. Her wings are no longer under her control. She comes to realize she's about to pass out.

There are any number of disasters which can befall your average bee. The most common to readers of this journal will undoubtedly be the fate of the garden variety garden bee unfortunate enough to be caught between a pane of glass and the metal screen in your typical North American window treatment. I'm sure most of you have occupied some time during your life staring at this poor creature as it bounces off the glass or off the screen desperately searching for a way out of its predicament.

As a young child you undoubtedly had a considerable amount of pity for the poor insect. You might even have gone so far as to open the window so the bee might discover easy egress. As you grew into a young teenager or some age thereabouts, you probably let the bee remain in this most uncomfortable of situations as you exerted your power over one of the few living things a young child is capable of exerting power over.

As you matured into an adult you certainly must have felt compassion for this living thing who, like yourself, was stuck in the most accessible of existential metaphors. Depending upon your temperament you either let the bee fly away, kept the status at its quo, knowing the probability of the bee expiring in the window was rather high, or through the use of any number of easily accessible household objects, you might have flattened the bee against the wooden window frame in order to eliminate from the world another predator upon mankind who might one day end up stinging either yourself or one of your loved ones.

Your choice. You tell me how you want this poor insect to wind up. The choice is up to you. From this point on, your decision will dictate the final result. Is it life or death for the bees? Will this story have a happy or a sad ending. You make the choice. Life or Death? Decide now, a great deal hangs in the balance.

Make up your mind.

We'll wait a little longer.

Need a decision.

Can't wait any longer.

Good choice! Glad you made the right decision.

The walking/talking mammal takes his seat upon the throne.

ANOTHER PRECINCT HEARD FROM

Where do you suppose we might find the Ghost of Pope John Paul I at this moment? An entirely pertinent question. When last encountered he was searching the airwaves for his wayward ward by means of gigantic leaps of faith in the transmission facilities of the U.S.A.P.S..

Unfortunately for the late great prelate, he is showing signs of being far too late and not all that great in the his newest sport, sideband locomotion. Along with a skewed concept of time which goes hand in hand with the cessation of life, the Ghost of Pope John Paul I has taken an interest in styles of existence which were completely foreign to him during his time among the quick. He's been touring the homes of thousands of U.S.A.P.S. prime time viewers and has misplaced the intent for originating this journey amid the deepest recesses of his unconscious.

The Ghost of Pope John Paul I remembers the faces of the many citizens he's encountered. Families. Unattended children staring into the flashing screen for hours on end waiting for anyone to come back into their lives and interrupt their electronically opiated existence. Loners sitting in rooms by themselves wondering how they came to be in such a solitary cell. Couples ignoring the electronic presence but using the sound waves to mask and add local color to their lovemaking. Old ones still marvelling over the fact that so many different people can come into their lives without their having to move from their comfortable chairs. As the Ghost of Pope John Paul I whips through citizens homes like a Nielsen man on amphetamines, there are far too many human lives and situations for him to digest.

While still among the quick, the Ghost of Pope John Paul I knew life was complicated but even with all the Machiavellian schemes swirling around him during the brief span during which he was the target of every red draped de-facto eunuch within his organization, his experiences were basically limited to those matters of everyday life which his flock voluntarily brought to him. This new form of information gathering presents the Ghost of Pope John Paul I with data far too alien for his intellect to fully digest without shutting down other portions of his brain, some portions which concern remembering what his purpose in existence is at the moment.

Puzzles. Puzzles within puzzles within enigmas within imploding palindromes.

The Ghost of Pope John Paul I was trained as a steward. A shepherd. A leader of men and women. He wasn't meant to get down in the ditches with the troops and administer first aid. The Ghost of Pope John Paul I is the ghost of a general. He directs how the troops should deploy. How the aid should be brought to those most in need. He made sure the ship of church continued on its chartered course.

-Too many people. Too many people all crammed together. And this in the U.S.A.P.S..-

The Ghost of Pope John Paul I is seeing his people as he'd never seen them before in his life or afterlife. He saw them in the hundreds of thousands. For month after month he flickers from Sony to Sharp to Samsung to Sanyo and even to the few decaying black and white sets long ago manufactured domestically. He remembers one named Phil-something.

-This is a politicians dream. Visiting the constituents. But the cost of admission is too high for most of them.-

The Ghost of Pope John Paul I prefers a more statesmanlike role. He's not on this mission to glad hand the great unwashed. He's not certain why he's on this mission but he knows he's on it for what must be a reasonable reason.

Some of the people he's observed are similar to those he knew while among the quick. Poverty reaches everywhere. But what is confusing to him is the extent of crowding within the cities of the U.S.A.P.S..

He'd enter an apartment and see seven or eight people crowded about the television screen. The Ghost of Pope John Paul I understands the room is not the gathering place for an extended family. This is an immediate family and they aren't gathered together in one room by choice.

On his first few visits to homes suffering from such overcrowding, the Ghost of Pope John Paul I took prevailing conditions somewhat in stride. Feelings of extreme empathy, which were formerly one of his great weaknesses, swept through his being. But the stimuli from other more affluent homes kept the overcrowding of the less fortunate demographic areas assigned to the portion of his consciousness labeled, "The Poor Are Always With Us."

What eventually effects the Ghost of Pope John Paul I is the increasing percentage of destitution. As he flits from screen to screen across the U.S.A.P.S., he begins honing in major population centers. As he began his trek eastward across the land, the elongated landscape and relatively sparse population disguised the prevailing circumstances, but as he zooms in on the older urban (no relation to former titleholders) centers, there is but a single assumption he can draw.

Thinking back upon his time among the quick, the Ghost of Pope John Paul I understands that too much of his precious time was employed in preparation. He'd prepared himself for the final office where he was certain he'd be capable of accomplishment. To truly help those most needy. To bring those responsible to task for the grievous ills being perpetrated against those most in need of compassion and support. Together with a few other leaders he'd outlined his plan. His ascendence to the throne would be the signal to all his collaborators to make their moves within their individual countries. This was the thought which predominated his consciousness as the future Ghost of Pope John Paul I took title to the most well known title in the world.

As the Ghost of Pope John Paul I went to bed that evening, he was aware that the forces of change were about in the world. He knew nothing would change overnight. He knew he had to keep hold of the reins of power as long possible in order for his cohorts to complete their varied tasks. The Ghost of Pope John Paul I knew his job was to remain Pope as long as possible.

So much for preplanning.

LIVE BUT REMOTE

It ends the way it began, in a field just west of northwestern Massachusetts. Snow falls. The army of "killer bees" approaches bearing a heavy burden for use in future negotiations. The media descends.

"It's been years since the surrounding Albany area has seen such an assemblage of non-uniformed armies descend upon their town. Various organized fringe elements have already staked their claims on the surrounding hillsides. Last night, the "Civilized Earth First, Last and Foremost" organization proclaimed the area to be a "Weedeater Zone" and now we can see a few of these well-armed neo-ecoconservatives members poking their heads out of their hastily built, yet heavily fortified bunkers.

"We spoke with one of "Civilized Earth First, Last and Foremost"'s leaders, a Mr. Omar, earlier this morning."

Go to clip.

"No bees. This field here is where the forces of "Earth, First Last and Foremost" have decided to stem the tide of alien bees. We have seen too much of the civilization we have worked tirelessly to create wantonly destroyed by the savage forces of nature left unrestrained. Property values have plummeted. Here we stand. Death to all infidel bees."

"This is the prevailing sentiment of the crowd out here this morning. It appears the citizens of the greater Albany area have drawn a line in the field and are refusing to retreat in the face of the massive swarm which according to latest reports is now less than a mile from our present position. I'll return you now to the studio. Stay tuned for further reports as this most ominous of situations develops."

Instantaneously the image of the compact human entity is lost from the screen and is replaced by a test pattern which fails to hold the interest of fifteen percent of the viewing audience who, not caring to wait the eventual ten minutes before "Midday Albany" resumes its special live broadcast of the "Killer Bees Invade the Capital Area Special", switch channels in the everlasting hope of locating a rerun featuring one of their favorite stars.

As the test pattern comes in and out of focus while the technoids back at the studio try to figure out how they lost control following what should have been a simple transfer from remote feed, the three hundred members of the home audience who still think test patterns are neat and have remained glued to their screens are treated to a short sermon by the former Bishop of Rome.

It's took the Ghost of Pope John Paul I quite a few thousand miles to figure out how to transform his means of locomotion into a transmission signal but he eventually did. After becoming exceedingly ill from having to view the insides of countless U.S.A.P.S. homes, he much preferred the old method when most of what he learned of the human experience came from folks chatting to him in a dark box. First hand experience has radicalized the post prelate.

The Ghost of Pope John Paul I knew it was time for him to make a statement and the fact that he is now occupying the same wavelength as his ex-parolee fills him with a certain humble satisfaction. It had taken him far too long to zoom in on the limited broadcast area of "Midday Albany" but now that he's here, he's ready.

Imelda is having a fine time chatting up her guests and her audience, all the while remaining oblivious to the reality of her show no longer being on either the air or cablewaves. Big Aloysius in his role as expert commentator is ably responding to most of Her Swellness's questions while at the same time periodically flashing a Polaroid of Little Aloysius at the lens. An earlier guest, J.D. Pynchon, with his cooking segment already completed, perches on the end of the couch, his face obscured by his left arm.

"Bees, bees, bees, bees, bees. Isn't it all too too. Wonderful. Yes. Thank you so very much, Mr. Aloysius, by good friend, for telling us all we have nothing to worry about from these friendly bees. Remember where you heard this tremendous news. We'll be back. Yes, we will."

And into the commercial which the station will have to make good at a later time since the test pattern still predominates the screen but is rapidly losing out to an ever stronger signal emanating from the Ghost of Pope John Paul I.

It's been a while since the wily prelate has spoken in public. At least he thinks it's been a while. In his present state he can't be too sure. But he's held a lot of what he's about to say inside himself for most of his conscious life and the Ghost of Pope John Paul I knows that this time his words will have true meaning. This time what he has to say will have some effect. This time he's not only going to be on local Albany television but he's pretty sure he's going to make the national cable hookup.

The Ghost of Pope John Paul I starts slowly, recapitulating the sights he's seen on his vast transcontinental voyage. He eviscerates major portions of the U.S.A.P.S. for helping to stifle the vox populi by disenfranchising so many of its people by letting the plagues of poverty, drugs, and illiteracy run rampant through a nation which the creator has blessed with so much.

Three hundred members of the viewing audience who thought they would be enjoying the endless pleasure of a simple test pattern sit riveted to their seats as the spectral image of the Ghost of Pope John Paul I raises holy hell.

The Ghost of Pope John Paul I continues his tirade. He mentions how he once was a member of the worldwide ruling elite. He brings to task certain members of the present government of the U.S.A.P.S.. He hopes to launch several grand juries as he tells the untold story of the invasions of Granada, Panama and the Bronx. He can almost imagine the President of the U.S.A.P.S. packing his bags to leave town at this very moment.

But the Ghost of Pope John Paul I doesn't stop there. there's more to be told. He isn't content to merely spill the beans on the present abusers of the public trust. Hoffa. He tells the audience of three hundred exactly what yard marker to search under in at the Meadowlands. The chosen three hundred are told the location of the bank and exactly which safety deposit box holds the complete set of Zapruda outtakes. The Ghost of Pope John Paul I recites the entire contents of the Fatima letter. All this and more.

He forgives Imelda for being such a flaming bozo. He understands that having to live in Albany is about as bad as it can get.

Three hundred viewers hear the words. One viewer gets the entire performance on video tape, unfortunately the cassette is later used to record a rare episode of "Barney Miller" and the Ghost of

Pope John Paul I's performance is lost for posterity. But three hundred hear his words first hand.

Of the three hundred members of the audience only two understand Italian well enough to comprehend what the Ghost of Pope John Paul I has said. Only two have really heard him. He was upset and forgot. In lieu of any bad Italian jokes at this juncture, you can imagine a scene for yourself. I'll supply the dialogue.

"What'd I tell ya about that Hoffa guy? What'd I tell ya?"

But all is not lost. In this forest, the tree does fall.

"And welcome back. As you can see, the "Killer Bees" have arrived. Imelda."

"Thank you, compact human entity. Mr. Aloysius, you like these bees, no?

"They've never done anything to hurt me. That's all I know about the subject. Has anyone in the viewing audience seen this dog?"

The other guest turns his back on the audience.

"Imelda, we're seeing something rather unusual. The bees seem to have a human hostage. Yes, I can see it clearly now. The swarm is less than fifty yards away. I can't tell how much of this the camera is picking up. The bees have taken the man, yes I can say it definitely is a man, and placed him, he's sitting in some kind of a chair, directly in front of our cameras. The hostage seems to be trying to say something. I can't hear it. The noise from the swarm is far too deafening. But he is trying to say something."

Cut to commercial.

SHOWTIME

The studio is lit up like the scene of a multi-car, multi-lane traffic accident on the interstate where thousands of inner city spectators show up to enjoy the show. On a hot summer night. When the humidity hovers over 90% and everybody in the city needs to break out of their apartments and be somewhere where it's cool and they can feel the sea breeze and can remember the reason why they bother to live in such an inhospitable place as New York City. That's the way the studio is lit. Unfortunately, the studio is in Albany and no one in the studio has the slightest idea what they're doing.

For months "Midday Albany" maintained its place as the number one choice in its timeslot on unaffiliated cable stations throughout the country. Reaching an audience estimated to be somewhere in the twelve to fifteen million range, the two co-hosts were cover stories for numerous fanzines masquerading as newsmagazines, and made their separate tours of competing talk shows discussing exactly how much trash should be allowed on trash talk shows which make most of their living interviewing other trash talk show hosts.

They wowed them on "Oprah". They kicked ass on "Donahue". Sally Jesse Whoever was left speechless. There was simply no way for any of them to respond to these two noble newshounds who came up with the idea for the "Honey of a Computer/Microwave Oven/Days of Our Hives" combination.

How they managed to create this breakthrough household appliance/daytime drama is another story entirely and undoubtedly it never will be fully told. Suffice it to say after the Former First Lady of the Philippines and Surrounding Suburbs renegotiated her contract, after changing her management team, after tossing out every stitch of clothing the tacky woman from wardrobe had foisted upon her during the early days of the show, Imelda and the compact human entity entered their adjoining offices one morning to find a swarm of bees hovering around the cable network scheduling board.

Imelda, well adapted to taking orders from just about anybody, was more amenable to the new regime than the compact human entity and became the spokesperson for the "Midday Albany" team. The bees by now had progressed enough to originate their own television signal using a minimum of two hundred and fifty-six of their swarm (five hundred and twelve for VGA color) and in a fashion similar to Max Headroom (who they have taken for their corporate mascot and living image), every morning the bees would pass along the corporate commands through the Former First Lady of the Philippines and Surrounding Suburbs, Imelda Marcos.

For the first time in her life Imelda tastes complete power. For many years she's had to watch her back, making sure she pushed the representatives of the U.S.A.P.S. far enough so they gave up the last dollar they were authorized to spend, but never far enough to make them wish for a democratic regime. It was a tough job but someone with a real fashion sense had to do it.

Now she's in a position where she doesn't have to cater to anyone. If she submits a report through the new C.E.O., General Sarnoff Toewhat, to a swarm of bees at the end of each month, it's a small enough payment for the power they invest in her hands, her petite and dainty hands.

Two dogs scamper in the sky high above us all.

www.ingramcontent.com/pod-product-compliance
Lightning Source LLC
Chambersburg PA
CBHW050510260626
47157CB00004B/1259